GAMBLER'S GUN

Center Point
Large Print

Also by John Hunter and available from
Center Point Large Print:

This Range Is Mine

GAMBLER'S GUN

JOHN HUNTER

CENTER POINT LARGE PRINT
THORNDIKE, MAINE

This Center Point Large Print edition
is published in the year 2025 by arrangement with
Golden West Inc.

Copyright © 1973 by John Hunter
Renewed copyright © 2001 by John Hunter,
pseud. for W. T. Ballard.

All rights reserved.

The text of this Large Print edition is unabridged.
In other aspects, this book may vary
from the original edition.
Printed in the United States of America
on permanent paper sourced using
environmentally responsible foresting methods.
Set in 16-point Times New Roman type.

ISBN: 979-8-89164-490-8

The Library of Congress has cataloged this record
under Library of Congress Control Number: 2024949774

GAMBLER'S GUN

CHAPTER ONE

My hometown, Silver, in Arizona Territory, was hot, gritty, stinking as any mining community stinks with the dust of new-mined ore. Oddly, it was not named for the metal found in the area, but for Jonathan Silver, who located and developed the J. Silver Mine and established the town to work it. The coincidence was the town's first joke and Jonathan laughed harder than anyone, because it was his mine. In my childhood it had been a sober, well-run, safe community. The only excitement for a boy was in the noise of the regular Saturday night blowoff brawls of miners bored by their week's work. As marshal, my father tolerated these battles but kept them within the bounds of moderation.

Riding into Main Street with Bud Gilbert, who towed our pack horse, just enough ahead of him to see to both sides, I looked for change but saw little. We had been gone over six years and I was torn two ways, part of my mind expecting the place to be different and part expecting it to be the same as if I had been away only overnight.

We saw few new buildings, many strangers on the street, and some people I recognized, but we were travel-stained and needed shaves and it was no wonder they did not remember us. Neither had the ranchers we had passed in the cattle country that surrounded Silver.

We reached the intersection of Mine Road and pulled up at the hitch rail in front of Miss Maggie's Concert Saloon, which the proprietor was said to have named to evoke the joys and temptations of the deadfalls that lined Pacific Street in San Francisco. We stopped there first to look for my father.

It might seem strange to look for a marshal in a saloon in the afternoon, before the gathering evening trade might take him there professionally, but Rob Stewart's greatest pleasure was in playing a piano, and Miss Maggie had the only one in town. Earlier than my memory went back he had established a habit of visiting the Concert, as it was called locally, before the Professor (who played for the later dancing and entertainment) was due, to spend a couple of hours making his own music, his long, slim hands sure and supple on the keys. To those uninitiated who found it a foppish pastime for a man it was explained that this was practice to keep his fingers limbered and ready for the times when he needed them quick and expert to handle a gun. He had a wide reputation as an artist in the use of firearms. I never had heard where he learned to play. My father was not a man to talk about himself. In fact, aside from my own experiences with him I knew very little of him. But by the time I was fourteen he had taught me to play on this same piano.

Bud Gilbert and I swung down, tied the animals, ducked under the hitch rail, and came up onto the raised wooden sidewalk. No sounds from the tinny piano came from behind the batwing doors. I pulled out the watch I had won in Dallas and saw that it was two-fifteen, a sluggish hour in Silver. The day shift was in the mine and those riders and ranchers who supplied themselves from the stores had come and gone. The town dozed until evening cool and the end of the mining day would bring it alive again. There were few people on the sidewalks, few horses scattered along the rails. Bud wanted a drink first thing to cut the dust in his throat and headed straight into the saloon. I was right behind him, putting up a hand to catch the shutters he let flap before they could hit me in the chest.

After the sun glare I could not see the room immediately, but I remembered it. It was long, with an open stairway at the rear that went up to a balcony with a wooden picket railing. Several doors opened off the balcony to the girls' rooms—cubbyholes, to judge by the number in the available space. Beneath the balcony was a small stage where the piano sat. In front were the poker tables and a faro bank in the corner. When my eyes got used to the dim light I saw that the room was nearly empty. Four men played cards at one table, but their negligent attitude told me the game was unimportant. The bartender was alone, reading a limp magazine, and there was no one at the piano. I would have to look further for my father.

Bud was already bellying up, wanting the jump of a drink or two before he went to see his own father, who ran the tavern in the hotel two blocks on down Main Street. The bartender put aside his magazine and brought out a bottle and two glasses. Bud poured both full, and said conversationally, "Looks a little slow," and the bartender said, "Early," shrugged, and went back to his reading matter, which was apparently more interesting than the small talk of a pair of unfamiliar drop-ins. There was no sign of Miss Maggie or any of her girls, who usually slept until early evening and worked through most of the night. Bud rinsed his drink around his mouth, swallowed it, and poured another, smiling crookedly to himself as we stood, getting the feel of being on our feet. We had been in the saddle two weeks and it took a little adjusting to get over straddling a horse.

Bud chuckled. "Wonder what the old man will say when he sees me in town." He sounded easy, unworried.

Neil Gilbert was a huge redheaded Irishman with a red handlebar mustache that made me think of the spread of horns on one of the Texas steers we'd been herding. Bud did not take after him physically, being smaller and towheaded, more like his mother, who waited tables in the hotel dining room.

"You go find out," I said. "I'll go on to the office and see if mine's there. Meet you later."

Bud paid for the whiskey and we left Miss Maggie's together, got our horses, and separated, he heading down Main toward the tavern, I turning into Mine Road, past the bank on the corner and a couple of stores and the livery. The storekeepers and four town men were lined up in the shade under the sidewalk roof in chairs tipped back against the wall. They watched me go by, speculative, and a couple looked as if they thought they might know me but weren't sure. At the marshal's office I got down again and went in.

A stranger sat at the desk, a tall man with a longheaded, narrow face, grey eyes, and a yellow mustache stained at one end by tobacco, as if he smoked cigars down to the last inch. The grey eyes went over me, sleepy, with little interest, lifted to a focus four inches above my head.

"What can I do for you, sonny?"

He looked to be at least forty, maybe forty-five, but I was a full twenty-one. I had been on my own for the six years since Bud and I had run away to see the world. We had not seen the whole world but we'd been in most of the poker games between the Canadian border and the Rio

Grande, through the cattle and mining country. My father had taught me to play poker as soon as I could hold and read cards (the only intimate communication we had) as one of his ways of preparing me for adulthood. I had a natural aptitude for cards and I could deal with the best mechanics in the business. I did not exactly relish being called sonny, but I did not let the irritation show.

"You must be a new deputy," I said. "Where's my father?"

He leaned back and looked at me more closely. "Who might you be?"

I started to say Kid Stewart, then changed it to Sam. It had been a long time since anyone had called me Sam.

"Oh. You're Rob Stewart's boy?"

Impatience added itself to my irritation. I thought I had been explicit enough. "That's right," I said. "Where is he?"

He rocked forward and stood up, taller even than I had thought, and a veil dropped over the grey eyes, although he still did not look directly at me. "He . . . he ain't here anymore."

"Anymore?" Surprise made me repeat him. "What do you mean?"

"I—well, he left town. I'm the marshal now. Name's Howe."

He had turned jumpy, defensive. I wondered if there had been a political shakeup, if my father had lost his job and Howe felt guilty at stepping into it.

"How long has he been gone?"

"Ah, over a year, I guess. I don't know exactly."

"Do you know where he went?"

An unhappy flush colored the sallow cheeks and he cleared his throat. "I tell you, son, maybe you'd better ask somebody else. I didn't know him, never met him. He was gone before I got here."

I did not like the sound of it at all, but I was not going to get any more from Howe. I went out and untied my horse, thinking where to turn. I thought first of going to our house, asking Mrs. Goodbody, who had raised me. But if my father had left town it would not be our house any longer because he had only rented it. And Mrs. Goodbody would probably be gone too.

My next thought was of Jonathan Silver, who owned not only the mine but the hotel and the bank. As the town's foremost citizen he made his headquarters in the bank. I turned that way, feeling a wash of childhood dread. As a boy I had been terrified of Jonathan Silver, not only because of his exalted position but because he was a giant figure, tall, broad, and had gone corpulent after he quit swinging a pick. His belly looked even bigger because of the watch chain that spanned it, thick links of gold beaten out of the ore from his second mine, the Daphne. Furthermore, he had a foghorn voice that had felt to me like a club one time when my father had marched Bud Gilbert and me in to see him with our confession of guilt.

Bud and I were seven years old; we had stolen a flask of mercury from one of the mine sheds. It was great stuff to play with. You could dump it out in a puddle on a piece of paper, break it with your fingers into little squirming drops that looked alive and escaped when you tried to pick them up. Then you could lift the edges of the paper and it all ran back together, quaking and shining. You could silver a penny with it so that the coin looked almost like a dime. There were lots of ways to enjoy mercury. My father caught us in the middle of the fun. He asked where we had got it—knowing where, of course—and I knew better than to lie and told him we had found it in the shed. He towered over us, the star bright on his shirt, even more imposing as the symbol of the law than as my ruling parent, and spoke in a quiet, man-to-man tone.

"You took it from the shed. Was the door locked?"

I nodded dumbly.

"How did you get in?"

I told him there was a loose board at the back and we were exploring.

Bud tried to help me. He said feebly, "Nobody was using the stuff."

My father looked down on him. "You think that

made it all right to take it? You've got a bicycle, haven't you, Bud? Are you using it now?"

"Well, no. It's home."

"So it would be all right if someone took it?"

Bud gulped, turned red, and did not say anything more.

My father said to us both, "Have you any idea how much money that flask is worth?"

We shook our heads.

"Thirty-five to forty dollars."

He might as well have said a million. I could not have been more impressed. My allowance was a nickel a week. He looked at me.

"It is my duty to put thieves in jail."

That really scared me. The jail seldom held anything but drunks, but some of them could be mean. Then he went on.

"It is not fair to give you special treatment just because you're my son, so what I'd best do is take you down to Mr. Silver and see what charges he wants to prefer against you."

We took the flask to the bank, Bud and I, with my father on our heels. He made us tell the story ourselves, then we stood holding our breaths while the banker looked from us up at my father, and clamped a big hand over his lower face.

"What's this?" he said in that bull voice. "Our marshal's son is turning to crime?"

"Do you want them held for trial?" my father said.

Mr. Silver stood up, looking like a mountain rising from the sea, and walked a slow circle around us boys, peering down from his terrible height. He said "Hummph" several times, along with a continuing volcanic rumbling.

"First let me find out the extent of the loss," he said at last. "I'll have what's left in the flask measured."

He took it away and neither Bud nor I thought to wonder how mercury could be measured in a bank. It was a heavy year before he came back, wagging his head ponderously.

"One dollar and fifty cents' worth gone," he said, and scowled and worked his thick beard. "By rights I ought to prosecute."

It took him another year to stomp around his desk and lower himself into the chair and set the telltale flask before him and glower over it at Bud and me. I had a vision of spending the rest of my life in my father's jail.

"On the other hand," said Jonathan Silver, "in view of Marshal Stewart's fine, long reputation for keeping the peace in this town and his record of swift justice that has accounted for an unusually low number of criminal offenses, and whereas this malfeasance of his only son would tarnish that reputation if it were made public in a courtroom, I am inclined to consider a restitution of the value of the missing mercury, payable in cash by each of the culprits. That will amount to seventy-five cents from each of you." He stretched an open palm across the desk.

On the verge of rescue, I looked up in desperate hope to my father, but he cast me down again with a slow shake of his head.

"You will have to pay it yourselves," the marshal said.

Tears filled my eyes and blurred the hulking man who held my fate in his hand. "I haven't got seventy-five cents," I choked. "I only get a nickel a week."

"And you, Bud Gilbert?"

"Me neither. I get the same as him."

"Well then," the banker said, putting his elbows on the desk and making a steeple of his fingers, "I suggest you make the payment in installments. I will accept three cents a week for twenty-five weeks from each of you. Plus six percent interest on the unpaid balance."

By the time we walked out of there, free men but heavily in debt, I knew the value of money, and on the way home I was told the other burden I must carry on my shoulders.

"Remember what Mr. Silver said about a marshal's reputation," my father said. "A lawman must always be honest. If he accepts a bribe, if he in any way takes advantage of his office, if he does not live up to a high standard of behavior, he hurts not only his community but himself. He opens himself to blackmail and ruins his chance of doing his job. Nobody will believe anything he says. And if his son does not behave in the same honest way, he puts his father under suspicion as well as himself. Never let anyone get anything on you by which he can hold any power over you to make you do something you know is wrong. Now, I believe Mrs. Goodbody made a deep apple pie this morning. You go tell her I said you could each have a piece to help you digest what you've learned today."

As I grew into my teens the weight of being the marshal's son grew heavier. I wanted to get out from under his shadow. I wanted to be Sam Stewart, not Rob Stewart's boy. That was really why I ran away. Bud went with me because we were so close that he felt the same oppression.

The interior of the bank had not changed a bit from that awful first day I entered it. It was a deep room with a counter running along the west wall. There were three cashier windows, but only two were used except at a rush hour, one by Random, the teller, one by Carter, the cashier. Both glanced up as I came in, but when I did not stop at either window they went back to work. I went on toward the office at the rear. The door there was always open so that Mr. Silver could watch what went on in the front of his bank, and through it I could see that he was alone. He looked heavier and there was a bow to his shoulders now.

I stopped in the doorway and said, "See you a minute, Mr. Silver?"

By his expression I saw he had no idea who I was, and his "Why, yes?" was a question to prove it. I moved on to stand where I had stood that first time.

"I'm Sam Stewart."

His eyes did not believe me for a moment, then he accepted it, sank against the back of his chair and sighed. "Yes. You've been gone a long piece."

"I just got back. Where's my father?"

He showed surprise. "You don't know? Close the door." When I had done that he used his words as a swift surgical scalpel. "He's in Yuma prison."

The logical thing to my mind was that he had got a better job there. I said, "As warden?"

He moved his big head sideways. "No. He killed a man in New Mexico. Sit down, son."

I was already sinking into the customer's chair. Rob Stewart had killed several men in line of duty and no one had ever suggested putting him in prison. He was a well-known gun, but his whole life had been on the side of the law.

"You'd better tell me what happened," I said. "This doesn't make sense."

The old man's face crumpled together with distress. "I always liked Rob, admired him. He was a man you could trust, could depend on."

I did not argue that. I waited for the mystery I could not imagine to be disclosed. Silver rhythmically slapped his fingertips against the desk as though there were something he wanted to be that could not be.

"He should never have gotten mixed up with Laura Whitaker. So long as he stuck to Miss Maggie's girls he was all right, but when he started wanting that one the trouble began."

Laura Whitaker had been my teacher, a beautiful girl. I'd been in love with her and her firm admirer for the courage she had shown in taking a whip to boys twice her size time and again, but I had never been aware that my father knew she was alive. The only women I had ever known him to show attention to were Mrs. Goodbody, which was only a friendly employer-employee association, and as Silver said, the girls in the Concert, among whom he showed no favoritism.

I said, "What about Miss Whitaker?"

"Yes . . . you were away all that time. Well, two, maybe three years after you ran off there was a fight at the church social. Some of the miners got their skins full and decided to join the social. Laura Whitaker was there and a Cousin Jack grabbed her, pawed her, and she clawed his face. He like to tore her dress off. Rob Stewart buffaloed him and took her home. That started the friendship. It went on to where people were looking to see them get married. Then all hell busted loose. You never know what a turn things will take. A new gambler came to town—Doc Danby, the kind of handsome, putting-on-airs sort that women lose their heads over, and a slippery bastard. Two years ago, all of a sudden they up and eloped, Laura Whitaker and Doc Danby."

That a schoolteacher would run off with a gambler did not astonish me. In this territory gamblers had as good reputations as lawyers and were generally more honest.

Silver was shaking his head. "Your father took it hard, started drinking heavily. Then Mrs. Goodbody heard from her sister in Tucson that Laura was down there, had gotten pregnant and lost her baby. Seems Danby was in a poker game when her time came, not there to call the doctor, and she had the child alone. Laura nearly died herself. Danby deserted her, but he kept turning up to get money from her after she got well and went back to teaching. Mrs. Goodbody's sister wrote that after one of these visits Laura was so furious that she'd said, 'I'd just like to kill him,' and the letter writer thought she was probably capable of doing just that. Mrs. Goodbody showed the letter to your father and he stormed down here, turned in his resignation and borrowed two hundred dollars from me, and left town. A few days later we heard Danby had been shot in the back, and after his trial Rob was sent to Yuma."

All I could think of to say was, "Did you get your money back?"

"No, but forget it, he's got troubles enough."

I opened my money belt and laid ten gold pieces on the desk. His eyes widened a little, but he did not ask where I'd got them. If he had I wouldn't have told him.

CHAPTER TWO

Yuma Prison was known infamously as the Hell Hole all across the West. The most vicious collection of criminals behind bars was gathered there. Built of stone, it occupied a bluff of conglomerate pebble and cement-like ground on the point at the confluence of the Gila and Colorado rivers, and was enclosed in a high stockade, impregnable. Some of the cells were mere caves dug into the hillside, ventilated by air ducts drilled down from the top. Others were built in blocks around the paved yard, double-barred and open to the weather in all seasons, six men to a nine-by-six-foot cage. The whole complex was dominated by a tower on which a Gatling gun threatened any rebellion.

My mother had died in childbirth and Mrs. Goodbody had been a strict substitute. I think that without knowing it my father had resented my living when his wife died and that this showed itself in the unflagging insistence on my being perfect that finally made me bolt. I still felt the antagonism against him but I could not bear the idea of him freezing and roasting in that place of cruel horror.

Fortunately, I knew the sheriff of Yuma and he was willing to talk to the prison warden and arrange for me to see my father. I was taken to the mess hall, where those prisoners who were permitted to leave their cells ate at long rows of tables. I was left alone to wait in the barren room, to feel the dread and hopelessness that permeated the whole place concentrated here like some living evil, strangling me.

He came in between two guards, hard-mouthed, hard-eyed men, one carrying a shotgun. Rob Stewart stopped just inside the door and looked at me without expression. He had aged. I could not tell how much of it was the effect of a year in the Hell Hole and how much would be normal in six years, but it hurt, surprisingly. When the guards had backed out and locked the door he came forward and said in a tone as normal as if we had seen each other only minutes before, "Hello, Sam."

I got out the single word. "Hello."

"You're looking good."

"You aren't," I said. "How in hell could they convict you? I heard that nobody saw the murder."

"I confessed."

The shock made my voice rise. "You did a stupid thing like that? Why?"

A small curve of his lips mocked himself. "I was a law officer a long time. Remember?"

"Come on, I'm not sixteen years old anymore. I've been around some in between. The guy deserved what he got, so even you shouldn't be so stiff-necked. What made you confess?"

"The fact that I killed him." He tried to stare me down, but it was his tired, beaten eyes that dropped. "Do me a favor, Sam. Keep out of this. Go live your life. Forget me."

"Keep out of what?" I said it fast.

He stood a moment longer, straight-backed, his shoulders square, staring across me at the wall above my head. Then he pivoted and went back to the door that opened on the courtyard. "Guard. Guard. I'm ready."

The door opened and the guard motioned him through with his shotgun barrel. My father went out, never looking back, and turned the corner out of my sight.

I stayed a moment longer, looking at the empty doorway, then I went back to the warden's office. He stood beside the window, a blocky figure with a weary face and heavy jowls, black eyes, and a mouth like a steel trap. He said, "Get what you wanted?"

What I wanted was my father out of that stinking place of rot, but I wasn't going to get that by asking. I said, "I'd like a little information from you. He tells me he confessed. How many years did he get?"

"Ten. They made it manslaughter because of the confession."

"Has he heard from anyone since he's been

here? I mean, has he received any letters?"

The warden spat into the brass cuspidor beside his desk. "One letter once a month, regular. It's from a woman up in Lordsburg, name of Whitaker. She's the widow of the man he killed but she took her own name back. Never can figure out a woman, I can't. Can you?"

I said I could not, thanked him for his trouble and walked back down the trail along the side of the bluff to town. The stage left at noon and I was on it, heading east.

Lordsburg was not so much of a town that I had trouble locating Laura Whitaker. She was teaching school again. I found her in the three-room school-house at the west end of town. I sat quietly in the shade cast by the one-story building until she dismissed her class for the day. When the last of the kids had escaped down the dusty ribbon of the road, I went inside. She was working on papers at her desk and I was angered that she looked hardly any older than when I had last seen her. I was anything but in love with her now.

She looked up, startled, and I felt her uneasiness as she appraised me. I was wearing a cowboy's low-crowned hat, a colored shirt, butternut pants, and cowman's riding boots. It was the rig I traveled in. I might be a good professional gambler but I was at pains not to look like one.

"I'm Sam Stewart."

Her grey eyes widened. Her hair was yellow rather than golden. I suppose it always had been, but that was not the way I'd remembered it.

"Why, Sam. You're taller than your father."

I nodded.

"Where did you fall from?"

"I didn't fall. I came up from Yuma to see you." I watched her face, her eyes, as I said it but they did not change the way I expected. Instead I saw a restrained eagerness.

"Did you see your father? How is he?"

I was blunt. "Older. Hardnosed. Pretty grey."

Her white teeth caught her lower lip and marked it. Sadness filmed the grey eyes. "I wish I could do something. Anything to get him out. It was my fault that put him there."

I thought the same thing but I wanted to hear it from her. "What fault was that?"

"I should have married your father instead of Danby. But after I did marry I should never have said anything about my troubles to that woman . . . to anyone. I made my mistake and I should have handled it myself. I should have sent Bob away as soon as he came."

I still watched her closely. "He didn't kill Danby."

She drew in a loud breath. "Did he tell you that?"

"No."

"Then you know something I don't?"

"I know him. I know from his reaction when I talked to him. Danby deserved killing and not even my hardnosed father would choose to go to Yuma when no one could prove he did it. Also, Rob Stewart would never have shot a man in the back. What made him confess?"

She stared at me with her mouth open, shaking her head.

"What made him lie?" I insisted. "Are you sure you don't know?"

"Sam, I don't. He didn't tell me. How else could I know?"

"You would know if you killed your husband yourself."

I might as well have hit her with my fist. She slammed back in her chair, doubled her hand against her mouth and looked over it at me with eyes as wide open as they could go.

"Oh dear God. Sam, are you trying to tell me that Rob said he killed Doc Danby because he thought I did it?"

She could not be that good an actress. I was not as sure of her guilt now as I had been when I came to her.

"That's the only reason he would confess, isn't it?"

"But this is dreadful." She was working her hands together, kneading her fingers. "What in the world would make him think I killed Doc?

Or that if I did I'd stand by and let him take the blame? Oh, no."

"Oh yes," I said. "I don't know what the circumstances were, but I do know my father. He's in love with you, or he thinks he is, which comes to the same thing. If he thought there was any danger of you being locked up for your husband's murder he would assume the blame without question."

Her face was white now, drawn, and she put out her hands in pleading. "How frightful. If it's true."

"It's true all right." I said it without a shred of evidence. I had only a feeling, and the way my father had told me what he had done—brazenly, as if to countermand my questioning it—the way he had told me to stay out of it.

She stood up and looked as if she might run through the door. "Then we must do something, get him free. What can we do, Sam?"

I had come here despising her, to break her down, to drag her to justice, but suddenly I believed her and my mind looked for a new answer. Thinking aloud, I said, "If neither you nor my father killed Danby, who did?"

She shook her head. She did not know.

"Robbery?"

"The sheriff brought me his watch, his diamond ring, about fifty dollars. They were all in his pockets when he was found."

I ran my fingers through my hair. "Let's come at it from another direction. Think carefully. Was there any reason why my father should think you did it? Where were you when it happened?"

She sat down again and looked at the past and spoke slowly. "Rob Stewart came to the boarding house where I was staying, in the afternoon. I found him there when I got home from school. He asked me where Doc was, what the situation was then. I told him Doc was living in Tombstone but that he sometimes came to Tucson to get gambling money from me. Rob said I should leave and go with him back to Silver where Doc couldn't reach me, or if he came, where Rob could handle him. I wanted to but I told him I had a contract to teach for a year and it was only half over. Rob said he would talk to the board and get the contract abrogated and that I should go clean out my things from the school. We argued so long that it was nearly dark when I started, and it was dark when I left the school with what I kept there. On the road I met Doc looking for me. They'd told him at the boarding house where I'd gone.

"He said he had a deal on the fire that would make him rich and he shoved an envelope down the front of my dress and told me to keep it for him in a safe place. He was pretty drunk. I tried to reach the envelope and said I didn't want anything to do with it or with him. He turned nasty, slapped me in the face several times, so I started to run. He came after me but he stumbled and fell down and I didn't stop until I got home.

"Rob was back at the boarding house talking with my landlady and they both asked why I was running and out of breath. When I could tell them Rob rushed out to look for Doc. I didn't see him again that night. After a while the sheriff came and told me Rob was in jail, that he'd come to the courthouse and said he had killed Doc."

Her bewilderment was still in her face. "Doc was alive when I last saw him, swearing, cursing me, trying to get up. That was why I believed Rob's confession. I don't know what could have happened."

"Maybe," I said, "somebody else found Doc after you ran, and killed him, and when Rob got there he jumped to the conclusion that you had done it. When you let him go to trial without a protest he was convinced."

"But why, Sam? Why should he think I could kill anyone?"

"That letter to Mrs. Goodbody, that sent him to Tucson—did he tell you it quoted you as saying you would like to kill Doc? He probably thought you had reached the breaking point that night."

"Oh dear God! What a tragedy of misunderstanding. And after all this time, how could the real murderer be found?"

"There's a place to start," I said, "if you know where Danby was working at that time."

"Yes." It was a strong sound. "He was dealing faro in Tombstone, in the Turquoise Palace, working for James Markley and Bert Thorne, who own it."

"And he told you he had a deal going that would make him rich, and gave you an envelope to keep. There could be a connection. Did you look inside it? Did you keep it?"

She lifted her shoulders and spread her hands, without hope. "I looked, and I've got it, but it's only a photograph of a man, no one I know."

"Could I see it?"

"It's at home," she said, and hurried toward the door.

She took me to the small house she was renting and handed me the stiff cardboard picture. The face that smiled there was heavy, black-eyed, crowned with a thick shock of curly black hair. Any man who had spent time in southern Arizona during the last ten years would have recognized Curly Bill Brocious.

Brocious had drifted west out of Texas to the Tombstone area and become a leader in an arrogant, powerful gang of outlaws. With John Ringo, the Clantons, the McLowerys, and the rest they had terrorized both sides of the border, holding up stagecoaches, running off cattle, murdering Mexican smugglers who tried to run mule trains of gold and silver up across the line.

I turned the cardboard over. On the back was the photographer's stamp. It had been taken in Chihuahua City in Mexico and it was inscribed with a date. The date was the key to the puzzle. Curly Bill had been killed by Wyatt Earp in Arizona more than a year before the inscription on this picture.

CHAPTER THREE

Of all the toughs in those outlaw communities that pocked southern Arizona, Curly Bill had stood out as the one to fear most. After he had killed Marshal White in Tombstone he stayed clear of the town, but he did not leave the territory, feeling secure under the protection of the powerful group known as the Tucson Ring. The leaders of this ring were the contractors who supplied the army posts scattered across mountain and desert as protection for the whites against the Indians, and furnished the beef to the Indian agents that fed the reservations, largely with animals stolen below the border and smuggled north. The Ring owned the saloons, gambling, and whorehouses that sprang up in each new town. Regularly they bought the legislature and made sure no man appointed governor would stand in their way. Most of the wealth in the country thus drained into their pockets.

Then Curly Bill Brocious got himself killed. I remembered the exact date because it was the same day that Wyatt Earp left Tombstone. For several years the big United States Marshal, his brothers, and Doc Holliday had dominated that part of the country, but their luck had run out there. Morgan Earp had been killed, Virgil crippled for life, and Wyatt himself was under attack by the Democratic politicians in Prescott and Tucson who were out to bring him to trial for murder. So Wyatt, Doc Holliday, and four friends rode for Denver and the safety of a different jurisdiction.

They were heading for a noon stop at the little oasis of Iron Springs, but Curly Bill and a party of outlaws were already camped there. When Wyatt came in range Curly Bill stood up behind the bank that hid him and cut down. The Earp party turned tail and ran—except Wyatt, who stood his ground and shot it out, put a double shotgun blast in Curly's chest, and saw him fall out of sight. But with eight other outlaws potting holes in his hat and clothes Wyatt too backed off, miraculously not hit. That had been on March twenty-fifth in 1882. The Earp group rode on north, and a grave marked as Curly Bill's was left at Iron Springs.

Now it was 1885, and I carried a picture in my pocket of Curly Bill taken in Chihuahua, with June third, 1883, plainly written on its back, more than a year after the Iron Springs incident.

There could be two explanations. Either the photographer had made a mistake in his date by well over a year, which did not seem likely, or Curly Bill had survived the fight, played dead and decamped into Mexico. While I had been in Tombstone I had heard a vague rumor that he was down there, married to a Mexican rancher's pretty daughter, but I had put it down to romantic legend.

Now if part of the story was true and Doc Danby had come across the picture and ferreted out Curly Bill's hiding place and tried to blackmail him, it would account for Doc telling Laura he was going to get rich, and it could account for his murder. Curly Bill was not a man to stand still for blackmail by anybody.

I would, I decided, have to be very careful in how I tried to get wind of Brocious. It was impossible to go chasing blindly all over Mexico, so Tombstone or Tucson were the most likely places to look first. If Curly Bill was alive he would probably not have come north to get Danby himself but would have someone already up here do the killing for him, which would mean he must be in contact with at least one of his old crowd. Since the Ring that had protected him was centered in Tucson, I went there first.

The town was three-quarters Mexican, a warren of mud houses along narrow, crooked streets, with the Americans there living away from the old plaza. Billy Lee Parks' house was the biggest in the community, for Billy Lee was a major power in the Tucson Ring. He had first surfaced as an army sutler during the war, and when that was over he headed west looking for a spot where he could put his particular talents to best advantage. Besides a knack for politics these talents included murder, thievery, lying, and cheating, and the men who gravitated to him were the sweepings of the frontier. I thought that if anyone knew anything about Curly Bill it would be Billy Lee, although I did not expect him to tell me gratis.

I left my blanket roll at the Planter House and walked the three blocks of dust road to Billy's. The building looked more like a fortress than a home, with thick, windowless outer walls and a heavy, nail-studded plank gate.

There had been eight men with Curly Bill at Iron Springs. Some of them undoubtedly were dead, but there had to be someone left, someone I could get to. But if I stood any chance of getting that one to talk I had to qualify as an insider, and the quickest way to that was to win Billy Lee's blessing.

I hammered on the gate, then saw a bell dangling on a chain and shook it. The clapper gonged on the hot evening air with a ring that could be heard all across the town. A peep window opened and Harry Bedso's chalk-pale face showed behind it.

Bedso had been a friend of Ringo's before that outlaw got suicidally drunk and killed himself, but he had not been at Iron Springs when Curly Bill was supposedly shot. Still, it was a break to find him here because I had never met Billy Lee and I wasn't sure he would listen to me. Harry was a cattle thief, smuggler, and killer, rumored to have been with the party that ambushed a Mexican gold train in a canyon thereafter called Skeleton because of the hundreds of human and animal bones of bodies neither the outlaws nor anyone else bothered to bury.

I said, "Hello, Whitey."

He looked surprised, recognized me, and sounded friendly. "The Cactus Kid."

That was the name Doc Holliday had hung on me after a poker game that lasted three days. Doc had been disgusted that anyone as young as I was then could take him at cards and had complained that I was harder to handle than a cholla.

"What you doing way over here, Kid?"

"I want to see Parks."

He was surprised again. "Why? You never was one of the crowd."

"I might want to shoot him," I said, "but I'm here to save him some money."

His knife-blade mouth curved. "You always was a flip one, buster. It's a wonder someone hasn't shut your gab off."

"It's been tried. What about it, is Parks here?"

"He's here. Hold on."

The peep-hole closed and Harry unlocked the gate and pulled it open. I went through and tried a shot in the dark as he closed and locked up again.

"Say, Harry, weren't you at Iron Springs the day Earp killed Curly Bill?"

"Nope." He turned around to me. "I was right here. Why you asking?"

"Funny thing," I shrugged. "I just ran into a fellow up north who claimed he was there and told me Curly isn't dead."

Bedso cawed a laugh that sounded like a crow. "If he ain't he's sure invisible. The grave's there and nobody I know has seen him since. A lot of the boys are dead . . . Ringo, Indian Charlie, Stilwell . . . times is changing."

I was disappointed. I had hoped Bedso would know about Curly and I'd thought he might tell me because, oddly, he had appeared to like me whenever we had run across each other.

We were in a stone-paved courtyard around which the two-story house was built on three sides, with the upper rooms opening on a balcony reached by stairways at each corner of the U. It was not yet dark outside but big lamps in brackets along the edge of the balcony were already lighted and cast fiery light that made sharp shadows under the shrubbery below.

In a big chair at a table on the far side of the patio sat the fattest man I had ever seen, energetically busy with both hands. He had a huge bowl of chili and beans, shoveling the mix into him with a high stack of tortillas. He neither stopped nor looked up when Bedso came to the table with me behind him and said, "The Cactus Kid. He wants to see you."

Billy Lee rolled a flat tortilla into a cone, scooped it full, crammed the whole into a mouth like a draw purse, chomped on it, swallowed, emptied a bottle of Mexican beer after it, and belched magnificently. Then he gave Bedso his attention out of eyes so deeply buried in fat that their blue was hard to see.

"Who?"

"Me, the Cactus Kid." I stepped from behind Bedso.

The porky head swiveled on his shoulders. There did not seem to be any neck. Interest quickened in his rasping voice. "The one that killed Pat Summer up in Kansas?"

"Right." Pat had been a gunman out of Texas who tried to use a holdout on me in a poker game.

"Pretty good." The fat man's belch erupted again.

Bedso put in, "Earp said he's better than Doc Holliday."

Billy Lee Parks wrenched his chair around, lifting it by its arms and banging down, squirmed one massive buttock off the seat and worked himself upright on elephant legs. He spoke to Bedso.

"What's he want with me?"

If he wanted to play that triangle conversation game I'd go along. I had time to wait.

Bedso said, "He wants to save you some money."

Billy stumped around to face me directly and we looked each other over, then he began to chuckle. It shook every inch of him like a dish of jelly.

"That's a new dodge. Want to save me some money how?"

I had a good smile. It had gotten me through some tight places. "Let me take over the faro bank at the Turquoise Palace."

His chuckle stopped and his eyes squinted until I could barely see a pinpoint of light in them. "What makes you think I've got anything to do with the Palace?"

I kept smiling. "Jim Markley and Bert Thorne work for you."

"Who says so?"

I did not tell him Johnny Behan had. It might have got the sheriff into trouble. "A lot of people know it, Mr. Parks. The smart ones know nothing happens in the Territory unless you want it to."

"And why should I give you the faro bank?"

"As I said, to save you money."

"What's that mean?"

I widened my smile. "Even Eaton, who's been running it since Doc Danby died, is a crook. He's skimming the game, pocketing a third of the receipts above his fixed percentage."

The fat man's mouth turned down viciously. "Can you prove that?"

"If the take doesn't improve in my first week you can fire me."

Billy Lee peered at me a while longer, then spoke to Bedso. "What do you know about the Kid?"

"He's a wizard with cards, one of the best." Harry sounded as if he had built me himself. "I saw him beat hell out of Doc Holliday and there ain't many ever did that."

"But does he know faro?"

"I invented it," I said.

The chuckle shook the huge body again. "I'll say this much for you, you're not shy about blowing your own horn."

"The squeakiest wheel gets the grease."

"Philosopher too. All right, you get the bank, but the take has to come up by that third you mentioned or out you go. You expect me to back you?"

"I'll manage." I had two thousand dollars in my money belt. "Forty percent to the house, sixty to me."

"You'll have to settle the split with Bert Thorne."

I did not like that and I didn't want to tell him Thorne and I were not exactly friends. If I'd asked Thorne for the bank he'd have thrown me into the street, because I had a strong hunch that he was in league with Evan Eaton in knocking

42

down on the percentage the Tucson Ring drew from the gambling games in the Palace. But if I went to him with a note from Parks there wasn't a thing he could do to stop me.

I stayed to have a beer with the political boss, then went back to the hotel. In the morning I caught the eastbound train for Benson, to meet the stage for Tombstone.

At that time Tombstone was still roaring along. The water that would later kill the town had not yet been struck in the mine shafts, and the principal properties were working two shifts a day. The mills at Charleston and Contention were going strong. The stage brought me in on Tough Nut Street and dropped me at the corner of Fifth in front of the Russ House that Nellie Cashman ran.

Nellie was a more than handsome woman, her eyes large and dark, her crown of black hair parted in the middle framing a face a little longer than oval. She was in her late twenties or early thirties and why she had never married was a mystery. She had had offers aplenty and from wealthy men, owners of good mines, yet she had stayed single. She had run hotels and boarding houses all over the west and the most dangerous thing a man could do was try to take liberties with her. The miners worshiped her and protected her like a little sister. She was behind her desk when I walked in, and although I had been gone from Tombstone for two years she said at once,

"Welcome back, Mr. Stewart."

She had always called me Mr. Stewart, never Kid, with a propriety that was part of her insulation against familiarity. I said I was fine and she asked if I were going to stay or was just passing through. I told her I didn't know yet, signed the register, and took the key she handed down from the board. I lingered in the narrow lobby, looking it over to make sure no one was sitting in any of the high-backed chairs before I asked my question. Nellie Cashman had the reputation of being close-mouthed, of never repeating anything of what she heard or saw, but she was openly opposed to the criminal elements in all the camps. I felt safe in saying, "Do you remember when Wyatt Earp was supposed to have killed an outlaw called Curly Bill? Have you heard any talk to the contrary since?"

She raised her dark eyes in surprise, then said, "Not recently. At the time, the *Epitaph* printed the story as Mr. Earp wrote it to the paper, but the *Nugget* said the men with Bill claimed he was only wounded and had gone to Mexico." She gave a short, disapproving laugh. "If he is alive he'd best stay down there. There's a warrant still out for his arrest for murder. He was accused of holding up a train, killing the men running it, and robbing the mail and express. That makes it a

Federal offense, so his crooked friends in Tucson couldn't fix it for him."

I thanked her and took my blanket roll up the stairs. She had given me the room at the end of the hall, a room no different than any of the hundreds I had used around the west, though Tombstone was not like any town I knew. There was an excitement about it, an unpredictability, a feel of never knowing from one hour to the next what might happen. More men had been killed here than in Dodge City or any other of the cow towns. Only Virginia City in Montana might have known as much raw violence.

The air in the room was stale with old heat, old odors baked into the walls. I opened the window in spite of the wind that whirled dust up and in from the crowded street. The water in the pitcher on the commode was also stale and nearly hot. I stripped to the waist and washed off what I could of the grit and cinders accumulated on the train and stage, put on a fresh shirt, and went downstairs when the supper bell rang.

About twenty people had gathered at the long table, but Nellie saved a place for me at her left. She sat at the foot of the table nearest the kitchen door, where she could direct the three waitresses. The meal was served family style, great platters brought in of meat, potatoes, beans, even fresh vegetables, which were hard to come by in this desert land. Nellie's table was noted for the best good plain food in town. Tombstone boasted some famous restaurants with cuisines that equaled any in the country, but for the men who lived at Russ House the fare had to be more substantial and rib-sticking.

Five or six of these nodded to me as we sat down, and one asked if I had been away. I knew most of them, had seen them here or at a bar or poker table, but none of them were friends.

When the meal was almost finished, someone came in through the lobby doorway. I looked up to see Bud Gilbert stop there with his fists akimbo on his hips and a mock accusation on his face. Then he came forward. Nellie Cashman stood up, motioning a girl to clear her place, beckoning Bud to take her chair.

He shook his head, grinning at her. "Ma'am, I don't want your place."

"Nonsense," Nellie said with an eye on business. "I've about finished and I can eat my pie in the kitchen."

Bud hesitated until she had gone through the swinging door, then sat down, winking at the girl who set his fresh place. He pushed his face forward at me.

"What the devil's the idea of running off without me? I been chasing you from hell to breakfast."

I punched him on the arm. "You'd been gone from home for six years. Why should I drag you away just because my father was in trouble?"

He frowned, saying softly, "I heard about that. What do we do, bust him out?"

"From Yuma?"

"It can't be that tough." He was serious. I knew that if I said the word Bud would go up against every law officer in Arizona.

"It's tough enough." I thought of the stockade, the rock cells and thick double bars, the guard towers and the Gatling gun. Very few prisoners had ever escaped from Yuma, and most of those who made it outside were quickly captured by the Mojave Apaches living along the Colorado, who collected a hundred dollars for every fugitive they returned.

Bud shrugged lightly and went to work on his plate. I finished and lit a cigar to wait for him, and by the time he was through the other boarders had left. We had the long room to ourselves. While the girls cleared the table I told him in a low voice all that I had found out and what I suspected. At the end of it Bud chuckled.

"So you've got the picture, show it to the law. With the federal government wanting him they can get him extradited."

"What good does that do me? So he's alive—that alone doesn't connect him with Danby's murder."

"What do you think will?"

"I don't know yet. Somebody up here knows

some answers. I have to find out who it is."

"Perfectly simple. How do you do it?"

"Watch the mousehole here. I've got my credentials as one of Billy Lee's men and the toughs will start figuring I'm one of them. Sooner or later I'll get a break."

"You hope. And when you do, then what?"

"Find Curly Bill and get out of him who murdered Danby. He's safe where he is and I don't think he's such a loyal cuss that he wouldn't give me the man for a price."

"Maybe," Bud mused blandly, "we could save the price and win him in a poker game."

CHAPTER FOUR

It was still light outside, and although Tombstone was not as hot as most desert towns, it still baked. Allen Street was as busy as I remembered it, jammed from sidewalk to sidewalk with horses, wagons, carts, and carriages, and the board walks were so crowded it amounted to a fight to reach the doors of the saloon. Inside the big room of the Turquoise Palace it was worse, lined two deep along the bar with six bartenders hard at work. The poker tables were full, men milled in a crush around the roulette wheels, monte layouts, and the faro bank. I almost expected to see Earp's tall figure over the other heads and find Doc Holliday lounging at a table.

Bud Gilbert's hair under the brim of his flat-crowned hat looked almost white in the light of the flaring lamps. As always when we were in a crowd he walked ahead of me, his bigger bulk making a path, not too gentle in the way he used his wide shoulders. He generally made a double impression, first drawing angry sound from those not courteous enough to give way, then a quick cooling as they met the cold blue of his eyes.

Behind the bar as we came against it I saw Judo Nay. He recognized me and lifted a hand.

"Hi, Kid. Where you been so long?"

"Here and there," I said.

"Who's your friend?"

Bud laughed and reached across to shake hands. He and Nay had had many happy drunks together. Nay set out a bottle and glasses and before he could turn away to other customers I said, "Bert Thorne around?"

"In the office. You know the way."

I dropped a dollar on the counter but he shoved it back. "Nice to see you again. Don't believe everything you hear."

I winked at him and told Bud, "Wait while I see Thorne."

"I'd better go along," Bud objected. He did not like or trust the saloon owner.

"No, I'll be all right," I waved him off. I did not want Bud with me this time. Bert Thorne was not going to like my proposition and would undoubtedly say things that would light Bud's short fuse, and I didn't want trouble between them because I intended to use Bud as my lookout.

Nay held up a finger for me to wait while he served another man, then came back and leaned toward me. "You want to walk a little soft around Bert. He'll remember you were a friend of Holliday's, though I never saw how you could stand the bastard."

I grinned to myself. Doc had had a sardonic

sense of humor that rubbed a lot of people the wrong way, which was just what he intended, but I wouldn't argue it with Nay.

"He's a good poker player," I said, and left to make a slow detour to the office.

There were no changes there either. The big safe against the wall still stood open, glittering with gold and silver coins to bank the games. Thorne was not alone. His partner was with him, an Irishman with a craggy face not improved in the prize ring where he had started. His fleshy nose canted to one side and his left ear turned nearly inside out. Bert Thorne was a different animal, tall, dark, mustached, groomed to the point of vanity, and looking more like a solid banker than the devious politician he was. He was adding figures when I pushed the door open. He looked up expectant, then frowned.

"I thought we were rid of you."

James Markley blustered at me, "You've got nerve all right, showing up here after the way we ran out your pals."

I didn't say anything, just stood smiling at the red face and the dark one. The Earps had ridden away from Tombstone at a walk, defiant through the ranks of their enemies, and I meant my smile to gall them here. Then I closed the door and walked to the desk and handed Thorne my letter from Billy Lee Parks.

He took it suspiciously, opened and read it,

shoved it toward Markley and thrust an angry chin at me.

"Now how the hell did you work this little whizzer?"

"No whizzer." I lifted one shoulder, still smiling. "Billy Lee doesn't like the rooking the faro bank is giving him. He sent me over to see if I could boost his cut."

"Rooking?" Thorne pushed to his feet and roared at me. "You're a lying son of a—"

My fist stopped whatever he thought I was a son of. I don't like being called a liar. Thorne stumbled back, hit the safe door, and fell inside with stacks of coins spilling down over him. James Markley stood gaping, holding the letter, then one ham hand dropped toward his gun, but mine was already up on him, tilted toward his crooked nose.

"Relax, Markley," I said, "and tell him to mind his manners."

He relaxed and spread his meaty hands on the side of the desk well away from his holster. Bert Thorne wrestled out of the safe, scattering coins across the floor, and found his feet, feeling at the lump growing on his chin, gritting through his teeth that he'd kill me.

"You could try. But Billy Lee wouldn't like your doing that to his pet dealer."

His hot eyes hooded down at that possibility and his long fingers brushed dust from his coat.

I had won my point. I would get the bank, but it was a good thing this brash had come in the privacy of the office, for Bert Thorne had an arrogant pride to match the fertile wits that were said to hatch many of the schemes of the Tucson Ring. Now I had to make a peace of sorts.

"I'd say we're even." I made my tone reasonably friendly. "And there's no point in our fighting each other. Billy Lee knows your dealers and maybe you are knocking down on the faro bank . . ." He started to get mad again and I added quickly, "I don't give a damn one way or the other, but he wants it stopped. It will be easier if you cooperate. I'm taking over tonight."

He tried to stare me down, found it didn't work, opened his mouth, closed it, shrugged and said, "All right, all right. Come on."

He led me out of the office, leaving behind us a James Markley who had had not a word to say. I gave Bud Gilbert the eye as we passed the bar and he fell in with us. There were half a dozen players at the faro board and Thorne raised his voice above the high noise-level of the room, closing the game, telling the dealer that I was replacing him. Nobody seemed to appreciate the change. The players growled at the interruption. The dealer, a nervous, shifty-eyed man, looked puzzled, then angry. The lookout on the high stool at the end of the table was square, blocky, with powerful shoulders and big hands. He did not like the change any better than the others. As he came down from his perch he deliberately stumbled to fall against me hard. Instinctively I put out a hand to catch him, but Bud Gilbert reacted differently. He grabbed the collar of the man's white shirt and threw him back against the stool so hard that he dropped to his knees, rolled to crack his head against the wall and lay stunned until the dealer shook him and helped him to his feet.

That was the way we took over the faro bank at the Turquoise Palace, with no trouble at all.

Any number can play at a faro layout. They do not play against each other as in a house poker game, where the houseman deals and takes a cut of every pot to pay for the use of the table. Each faro player bets against the dealer, as much as he chooses. The layout behind which I seated myself was a table covered in green felt with a full suit of spades pasted on it face up. The ace is the card closest to the dealer and the row ends with the six. Seven turns the corner and the cards run upward from it to the king, which is opposite the ace.

I set out the coins from my money belt in ordered rows, shuffled the deck and put it face up in the shoe, a box without a cover. The top card, called the Soda, is thereby exposed.

"Gentlemen, the bank is open," I told the players. "Place your bets."

There are twenty-one different ways to make a faro bet. Money placed full on any of the pasted-down spades bets that card to win. A copper stacked on top of the bet plays the card to lose. Money placed between two cards bets either to win and is paid off half the value of the winner. Divided between three cards, any one of them winning pays a third, and quartering four cards is worth one fourth.

The skill in faro comes in keeping cases on, or remembering, what cards have been drawn and projecting which ones remain in the box to be uncovered.

I had played faro many times but always from the other side of the table. I looked up at Bud Gilbert, lounging easily on the high lookout chair. It was Bud's job to watch the actions of each player below him, some of whom were not above trying to move their bets after the cards had been turned. I waited until the flurry of hands placing coins was over, closed it by saying, "All bets down," and began the game.

The Soda was the queen of diamonds. I took it out of the box and laid it aside. Beneath it was the six of hearts. I took that out and put it face up beside the box. This card lost, but by removing it I uncovered the winner, the eight of clubs. Its matching number was the eight of spades and I paid off a bet there and collected the losers' money. Then new bets were put down and I removed the club eight from the box to expose the next winner.

The play got heavier, the stakes higher as the night wore on. At midnight I closed the game for half an hour, ate a sandwich and drank a cup of coffee that Bud brought me, then we changed places—he dealt and I watched.

At four-thirty the play fell off and I closed the game for the night. We had almost doubled the stake and we took the winnings to the office, counted out the house's forty percent, put our percentage in our money belts and headed up Tough Nut Street toward the Russ House.

Two blocks on our way a hoarse voice spoke out of the deep shadow of a store porch. "Put up your hands. This is a shotgun with buckshot and I'd love to cut you in two."

We stopped. There was light enough from the distant street lamps that we could be seen, but none under the porch roof. Even if we risked turning we would not know where to aim. The voice was tight, as if the man was under considerable excitement. I did not like that at all, didn't like standing in front of a shotgun when a nervous man had his finger on the trigger.

He spoke again, just as tense. "Lay down on your faces and stretch your arms out. Keep your nose down. Now."

I looked along the sidewalk. Even at this dead

hour there should be traffic on this street, but the only movement I could see was a pair of drunks a block ahead supporting each other, weaving through the dim light, going the same way we were, with their backs toward us. I lay down on my belly and stretched my hands along the boards, aware of Bud beside me doing the same, swearing under his breath.

Footsteps came off the porch—at least two men, three I thought—then hard metal, a gun barrel, shoved hard against the back of my neck. A hand I could not see pulled the gun out of my holster, snaked out my sleeve gun. I heard the guns broken and the soft splatter as the shells were thrown into the dusty street, then hands ripped my shirttail out and wrenched my money belt around until they could reach the buckle. I squirmed and the gun pushed harder in my neck. I lay still again. The belt was stripped out from under me and Bud grunted and I guessed he was losing his too.

"Stay right like you are for five minutes," the voice said, and the footsteps crossed the boards to the silent dust of the roadway. I couldn't tell whether they were gone or not until I heard horses running in the alley behind the buildings.

I got up slowly, bitterness in my mouth. It had all gone so well until now that I'd got careless, I had put too much trust in Billy Lee's letter to neutralize Bert Thorne. The knowledge didn't help anything. Bud was on his feet, gone to hunt our guns. He came back saying,

"They got it all, huh?"

"All but what's in my pants pocket. There goes the faro bank."

Bud had a nasty sense of humor. "Maybe Bert Thorne will back you," he said.

"Sure, sure. Did you recognize that voice? That was the dealer we shut out. I'd say it was a neat trick of Thorne's. With Billy Lee's letter he had to give me the bank, but without a stake how could I run it?"

"Go back to Billy Lee?"

I gave him a short laugh. "He'd tell me if I was stupid enough to let this happen I'm too stupid to handle the game. I'll have to find another way to get wind of Curly Bill."

We were moving on down the street, reloading our guns as we went. Bud was silent as he finished and shoved his holster full, then he said thoughtfully.

"Maybe Clum down at the *Epitaph* might have some ideas."

"Worth a try in the morning," I said, but I hadn't any real hope.

The *Tombstone Epitaph* was only one of the four papers published in town, but it seemed to me that its editor had a better grasp of things as they happened in the territory and a less florid fancy in his reporting. It was eleven o'clock when we walked in and found Clum in his cubbyhole office behind the print shop. He had been a good friend of Wyatt Earp and by extension he welcomed us back to town.

"What was that fracas about the faro bank at the Turquoise last night?" he wanted to know immediately.

"News does get around," I said. "And if I give you the whole story will you hold it until I say you can print it?"

He thought about that for a minute, his eyes narrowing, then he shrugged. "Depends on how good the story is and if you'll promise me an exclusive."

"It's an eye-popper if I'm right." I decided to trust him. "But if you blow it before I'm ready I'll come looking for you with a gun."

"That's been tried on me before and I'm still here, but let her rip."

I told him the whole thing, even to the robbery last night, and showed him the photograph of Curly Bill and pointed out the date on the back. His only sign of excitement was a low whistle, then a shout to the printer's devil.

"Hey, Petie, dig in the morgue and fetch me the story about Wyatt's and Curly Bill's brouhaha at Iron Springs. Be around March twenty-six back in eighty-two, or a day or so later."

When the boy brought the paper Clum read

it over, refreshing his memory, and gave me a twisted smile.

"Wyatt sure said he killed Curly and I never knew him to claim something he didn't do, but with all that lead flying I know he didn't go in and check. I thought that rascal's column over at the *Nugget* was some of his usual bull. It would be a laugh if for once he wrote the truth."

"I've got to find out," I said. "So where would you look for Curly?"

He raised his eyebrows in surprise. "Why, I think I'd go ask the photographer first."

My mouth dropped and Bud looked sheepish, then we began to laugh. The obvious, the utterly obvious—so obvious that neither of us had thought of it.

CHAPTER FIVE

The troubled land below the border had known no peace since it threw off the yoke of the Spanish king. One rebel leader after another had grabbed for power with a force of bandits at his back. Mexico had fought a losing war with the United States in which its northern provinces were cut away from it, but never in its history had it been in such turmoil as on the day Bud Gilbert and I crossed the river from El Paso. The Emperor installed by the French had died before a firing squad and the bandits who made up the bulk of Juarez's army were fighting among themselves. Any traveler stood a good chance of getting himself shot or robbed or both.

Bud and I weren't too worried. We were heavily armed, each with a rifle in a boot under our legs and two handguns, and for luck I carried a Greening on a swivel hung from my saddle horn. Each of us wore a pair of heavy cartridge bandoliers slung over our shoulders. As Bud said, all we didn't have was a Gatling gun or a howitzer.

We rode through the little collection of mud huts on the south side of the river known as Ciudad Juarez, and headed into the back country, not hurrying. We had nearly four hundred miles to go and the trails were bad, little more than traces in some places. The country looked desolate and empty, with everybody in hiding. People were frightened of the bands of former soldiers now roaming and raiding for anything they could steal, and terrified by the Apaches, who were breaking out of the northern reservations and sweeping the land far down into Mexico after horses and women and children for slaves.

We rode at night, with more caution than I had ever used in the States, and camped by day far off the trail, one of us standing guard while the other slept to avoid being surprised. Several times we heard parties of horsemen galloping past, but it was three days before we really came into contact with other human beings, and they were like ghosts.

We began to pass the buildings of ruined ranches, roofless, gutted by fire, their cattle and stores carted off and those peons left alive dazed, cowering helpless in the wreckage of the once-great haciendas, waiting for owners who had not returned.

There were ranches still operating, a number of them, that had the manpower and determination to stand off the raiders. To both pillaged and surviving we gave a wide berth. In this time of death and suspicion, no stranger was welcome within gunshot range.

Chihuahua, one of the foremost cities of

Mexico, had a bad case of the jitters and was an armed camp. Two regiments of Diaz's men were quartered there, ragtailed and underpaid, swaggering on the dirt streets that surrounded the government palace, half drunk and doubly dangerous. There was a surprising number of Americans, watchful men who crossed a road rather than meet a countryman face to face.

There was an American consul, but as soon as he saw us, before we could speak, he said flatly that if we were in trouble there was nothing he could do to help. We had not expected the kind of help he was talking about. We showed him the back of the photograph and asked where we could find the photographer. In painful relief he led us to the door and pointed out a small shop at the end of the street, well beyond the Plaza.

We rode toward it past the rough stone walls of the palace. Dangling above us in grisly decoration at the windows were rows of Apache scalps, brought in through the years by scalp hunters. Some were so old that the skin had rotted and only tufts of the lank, coarse black hair remained to hang lifeless in the still, hot air. It had been twenty years since the Civil War had put a stop to the bounty hunting, but the authorities had left the things there as a reminder to any Apache who happened into town. Since Chihuahua was one of the few places in northern

Mexico that had not been attacked, it struck me as pointless, but it was not my business.

The shop was adobe, a single room divided by a curtain, with the rear used as living quarters. The photographer's name was Spanish, so it was a surprise to find him an American, sandy-haired, greying, with a long, dolorous face, his chin nearly down to his wishbone. He bowed us in like long-lost cousins and celebrated by breaking out glasses and pulque. I didn't like the fiery stuff but I wanted his help and took it rather than offend him. A garrulous soul, he rattled on while we drank, said he'd been in Chihuahua ever since the end of the war. He had been an army photographer on the Confederate side and after the surrender couldn't bring himself to go back to his native Georgia.

"Did you gentlemen want your portraits taken?" He was pathetically eager. "You'd be surprised at the number of Americans who come to me. Mostly they're men who for some or other reason can't go back, but they're homesick, so they send their pictures north."

Bud laughed. "Only one we might send back would go to the sheriff, and he's already got our faces up on his wall."

The man—his name was Moreno—was sympathetic. "Too bad, too bad. Then what may I do for you?"

I let Bud's joke stand; it just might do us some

good. "You took a picture of a friend of ours down here and we're trying to locate him."

I handed him the photograph and watched for his reaction. He showed no recognition, but he did go to a large wooden box in the corner, pull out a drawer, and lift out a stack of plates, each of them labeled. He sorted through them, found the one he wanted and brought it to us.

"Here we are," he consulted the label. "Mr. Brown. Mr. Mike Brown?"

"Yep, that's Brownie all right," Bud said happily.

I had not expected Curly Bill to be using his own name, but like many men who take an alias he had kept his initial, the B from Brocious. I almost held my breath for my next question.

"Do you know where he is now?"

"Why yes. He's foreman of the Livingstone Ranch."

"And where would that be?"

"Do you know where Galeana is?"

"No."

"North of here on the Santa Maria River. The ranch lies about ten miles from town."

I thought of the burned-out places we had passed up that way. "Is it still operating? I mean, with all the bandits and Apaches, are the people still there?"

Moreno grunted, an ominous sound. "Nobody had better attack the Flying L. They've got a fighting crew, maybe fifty men. They run about quarter-million cattle and even the Mexican army is afraid to go in there."

That added up, of course. If indeed Curly Bill was foreman up there he would have gathered to him all the hardcases from both sides of the border. Curly Bill was a natural leader, soon dominating any group of which he became a part, and the no-man's-land that was the territory for a hundred miles south of the border was an ideal stage for his kind of operations.

"Who owns the ranch?"

"Anne Marie Livingstone."

"A woman?"

"Young woman. Her father, man called himself Lord Livingstone—though whether the title was real I can't say—he married into an old Spanish family and either wheedled or bought the ranch into his own name. He died last year and his daughter inherited it."

Bud raised his eyebrows at me. To hear that Curly Bill was foreman for a young woman was interesting to say the least, considering his reputation among the saloon girls at Charleston and Contention. It rather put his Lordship's daughter's character in question.

"Thanks," I said. "Now how's the best way to get there?"

Moreno hesitated, very uncomfortable, then he blurted, "Unless you're very good friends indeed I'd advise you not to go. They don't like strangers."

Bud Gilbert hitched his shoulders. "We ain't strangers. Fact is, Brownie's my cousin . . . cousin first removed, as we say in Missouri . . . Brown's my name."

Bud made a game of lying; it was his favorite form of entertainment, his way of laughing at the world.

Moreno still sounded dubious. "Well . . . you take the El Paso road north to El Sueco, then go west through Flores Magnon and on to Galeana. Anybody there can tell you how to find the ranch . . . if you're sure of your welcome . . ."

I was not at all sure of our welcome. When we had turned around and headed back the way we'd just come I told Bud, "I hope Mr. Mike Brown is agreeable to finding he's got a cousin once removed from Missouri. One of these days you're going to get stuck with a lie and have a time getting out of it."

He laughed at me. "It got our information, didn't it? But hell, I wish we'd known where we were going when we started. We've come anyhow four hundred miles out of our way. I love to ride for the sport of it. Can't think of anything I'd rather do than spend a month in a nice soft saddle."

I didn't pay much attention to his chatter. I had a problem to figure out. If Curly Bill had fifty hardcase riders, how were we going to get him away from the ranch and across the border? Because even if he told us who he'd hired to kill Doc Danby, we wouldn't be believed unless he told the authorities himself. Finally I broke in on Bud and asked if he had any ideas. He grinned at me.

"Promise him something he wants."

"Like what? Dancing girls?"

"Like a shipment of half a million dollars' worth of gold for the taking."

I twisted in the saddle to look at him. "I don't know anything about any half-million gold shipment."

"Neither do I. But Curly Bill doesn't know that. We can feed him a line about the gold coming through Benson on a certain day, get him up there, separate him from the crew he brings with him, and we'll be long gone before they find out there's nothing on the express car worth the trouble of holding it up."

"You've sure got a devious mind," I told him.

"Who was it thought up the bright idea of stealing that quicksilver your old man caught us with? Me or you?"

There wasn't any point in going on like that, and we rode through the night with less talk. As dawn spread across the east we pulled off the road, found a place to hide the horses behind a boulder pile, and spread our blankets. I took the first watch and had to keep kicking Bud. The way he snored he could give us away to anyone half a mile off.

About noon I saw a party of horsemen coming up the trail. They stopped at a cluster of big rocks and pulled off the track but did not dismount, only kept watching up the road. Then I saw two riders coming the other way, a man and a woman. At the distance I could not have told it was a woman except that her hat hung down her back on a chin strap and her hair fell shoulder-length, bright gold in the sun.

As I watched, the group of men separated as though to let the pair ride between them, then suddenly closed around them and one grabbed the woman's bridle. Her hand flashed up and her quirt caught the man across the face. He dropped the bridle and swung his arm to protect his face. The woman drove in her spurs and galloped away from the road, straight toward where I sat. I heard a shot and the man with her went out of his saddle and sprawled in the road and lay quiet.

I kicked Bud hard. "Company coming. Roust out."

I stood up, holding my rifle ready. The woman did not see me, looking over her shoulder at the half-dozen men driving after her.

I shouted in Spanish, "Over here. This way. I'll cover you."

She looked toward me, hesitated, then leaned

forward and spurred toward me, and as she came closer I saw she was more girl than woman. Bud had come up at my side with his rifle and stood smacking his lips.

"My oh my, see what the Lord done brought for me."

The girl slid her horse to a stop abreast of us and the men came on. I put a shot over their heads by way of warning. I don't think they were aware of us until then, but the shot brought them wheeling to a stop, milling in uncertainty. I spoke over my shoulder to the girl in the saddle above me.

"Who are they?"

"Soldiers . . . bandits . . . what's the difference?" Her voice was bitter. "It's all the same in Mexico nowadays."

"What do they want?"

She sounded not as frightened as contemptuous. "To rob me, hold me for ransom. To rape me perhaps. Who are you?"

"Just a couple of American travelers."

She switched to English. "You made a mistake, helping me. They won't forgive you."

I had turned my head to look at her and Bud coughed. "Time we clear out of here, folks."

I looked back and saw what he meant. Three of the men were dropping out of their saddles, pulling carbines from their boots. The others were riding out of range to flank us.

"Get the horses," I said. "Never mind the camp. We can come back later."

Bud ran to throw the saddles on the animals while I held off the attackers. I put one bullet through the shoulder of the nearest man and saw him spin and fall. I fired at a second man as he raised his carbine. He shot at the same time and his slug whined over my head.

The flankers were firing now, and I had my hands full trying to stand off both groups. The girl showed no excitement, had pulled a small revolver and sat calmly firing. She might as well have used a pop gun—her lead would not carry far enough—but between us we did discourage a rush.

Then Bud was there, yelling at me to mount up, shooting to cover me as I did. The girl wheeled and pounded away over the rolling ground, with Bud and me on her heels, firing back. Bud hit one horse and it went down, falling on top of its rider. The flankers hauled up and rode back to the group. Apparently, with two men down they no longer liked the odds. We ran half a mile before we eased the pace and let the horses blow.

"Now," the girl said imperiously, "I want to know about you two." It was hardly the tone you'd expect from someone we had just rescued from a fate no good girl admits to liking.

"I'm Sam Stewart. The ugly one with the cast in his eye is Bud Gilbert. Who are you?"

She ignored my question, studied Bud, then shook her head. "There's no cast. I want the truth."

Bud said, "He thinks that's a joke. I'm really a Spanish grandee in disguise, looking for some property an ancestor of mine mislaid a couple of centuries ago."

Her head went up defiantly. "I don't believe either of you. More likely you're a pair of American outlaws hiding down here."

"You guessed it." Bud grinned at her. "We stole all the gold from the Denver mint. If you're a nice girl we might give you a couple of bars."

She looked from one to the other of us, challenging, obviously a person used to giving orders and being taken seriously; then she bit her lip with very white teeth as a smile tried to spoil the effect.

"You're glib enough anyway, but I'd really like to know who to thank."

That sounded better, but Bud shook his head sadly. "If I did tell you the truth now you wouldn't believe me."

"Maybe. Try me."

"I'll trade you. I'll tell you if you'll tell us who we rescued."

"I will, but you first."

"Sam Stewart there," Bud said. "Called the Cactus Kid. He's a gambler, a gunfighter. I'm his backup man."

"Oh, now you're outrageous."

"See? I said you wouldn't believe. But it's true."

"Well . . . all right. I am Anne Marie Livingstone."

That kind of luck hits like lightning. I'd been wondering how a pair of strangers were going to get inside a ranch noted for not liking the uninvited, and here we had just done a favor for the owner herself.

"Of the Livingstone ranch?" I said to be sure.

She looked startled. "You've heard of it?"

"Who hasn't? It's a place I've always wanted to see."

"Then come along with me."

"We'd better pick up the gear we left back there first."

"Never mind. I'll send someone to bring it in."

CHAPTER SIX

It was a fifty-mile ride from where we met Anne Marie to the Livingstone ranch. Looking back from the top of the hill where we hauled up, we could see the dust of the attacking party, back on the road and heading away from us. I explained our reason for traveling at night to the girl and finally convinced her we should lay over until dark.

I asked her, "Don't you know it's dangerous to move around this country in daylight without an escort?"

Her head came up defiantly. "Of course I know. But this was an emergency and I had to risk it."

Bud squinted at her in suspicion. "I'd think as owner of that ranch you could afford to hire some protection, more than one man?"

"At this particular time in our country," she said in an icy voice, "one is likely to be safer with one person one knows than with a band of hired strangers who might decide a young woman was fair prey, don't you think?"

"Touché," Bud winced. "But you needn't be afraid of us. Where we come from a woman like you is up on a pedestal out of reach . . . So what's your emergency? Can we help?"

We were riding off the hill, getting off the

horses in a draw deep enough to hide them, and she didn't answer until we had the animals hobbled. She had tossed me her reins and sat on a boulder in the only shade there was, studying us through long curling lashes nearly closed.

"Why would you want to help? Gamblers, gunfighters . . . what are you doing down here?"

Bud's wide grin was easy and contagious. "Come south for our health, ma'am, like a lot of other Southerners—and we Missourians are noted for our gallantry. Ladies in distress are plumb irresistible. Just try us."

If looking at us the way she did could tell her anything about us, she read us like a book, but she finally lifted one shoulder, sighing.

"I may . . . after we get closer to home."

That was all we got from her that day. I slept on the hot sand while Bud watched, then he took a turn. Just before dark Anne Marie brought a canteen and her saddlebag and shared her water, tortillas, and jerked meat with us. Then we rode.

There was no moon, but starlight gave us enough to see by and keep our bearings. Although the girl did not know the country this far from the ranch any better than we, she said her spread lay west and a little north. It was rough land, cut by gullies, brutal with cactus, and the going was hard because we had to stay away from roads and trails where we might meet other night riders, raiding and marauding. It was after dawn before she began to recognize landmarks and made a shift in our heading. When she could see our faces she called a halt for a conference and we got down to rest the horses.

Standing beside her stirrup while she talked, she gave me the impression that she was poised to bolt if our reaction to anything she said raised her suspicion.

"Do you," she asked, "know an American outlaw named Mike Brown?"

Bud and I nodded warily. So the girl knew Brocious was an outlaw—and he was her foreman.

"Are you friends of his?"

Bud's laugh was dry. "We were in Wyatt Earp's camp. Broc . . . Brown didn't like the Earps. Why?"

"Are you afraid of him? He's got a crew of over fifty working for him—rustlers, murderers, robbers." Apparently she did not pick up Bud's near slip in the name.

I said, "It sounds to me like you want to get rid of them. You want us to go up against an army like that?"

"Not try to fight them, no . . . And that's the only kind of crew that could hold the ranch together in these times. He's a necessary evil. What I need is someone to protect my interests. I'll have to give you some history if you're to understand. Then you can decide."

What she told us was that the ranch had been a grant from the king of Spain almost two hundred years before, to her mother's family. Fifty leagues, about a quarter of a million acres. It came down to her grandfather, what was left of it after the revolutionists and Indians and American bandits had stolen enough to almost bankrupt the family and their neighbors.

Then the mother, Maria Teresa Gutierrez, married Douglas Livingstone, an Englishman who had brought a hell of a lot of money to Mexico with him. Anne Marie did not know the source of the money. Livingstone bought out the grandfather and three adjoining ranches, brought in the fighting crew from the American side, and began building his empire. Anne Marie grew up surrounded by outlaws, but her father had been a lot of man, had kept them in hand. They had made a mascot of the girl.

Then Brocious had come on the scene, been made foreman, and shortly afterward Livingstone and his wife had been caught in their buggy in a flash flood and drowned.

Anne Marie had inherited everything, but there was an Aunt Carmen on her mother's side who was furious at being left out of the will. So Carmen had moved in and married Curly Bill under the name Brown, and between them they were stealing Anne Marie blind.

The ranch shipped ten thousand cattle a year.

Curly Bill drove a herd to the border and sold it for beef for the Indian reservations, obviously through the Tucson Ring. Anne Marie, in checking over her father's books, had made the discovery that the money Mike Brown was turning over to her from sale of the herds was a lot less than when old Livingstone had been running the show, and when she had confronted him with her question why, he had passed it off as a result of the Texas depression.

"But you know Texas was depressed a long time before my father died," she finished. "I told Mike Brown I was going along on the next drive. Then I went to Chihuahua to visit friends. I'd been gone a week, expecting to stay a month, until near time for the next drive. But then Juan, one of our peons, came down to tell me Brown was already gathering the cattle and would start north in a few days, while I was away."

Bud raised his eyebrows at me, and I said to the girl, "So that ambush yesterday could have been something other than an accidental run-in?"

She said nothing for a long moment, slowly drawing in her breath, her back straightening, going rigid.

"I hadn't thought of that. Mike Brown is certainly capable of something on that order. Aunt Carmen . . . Well, Mike probably wouldn't tell her the truth. What . . . what in the world can I do now?"

"Put us on the payroll for the drive. We can look out for you, maybe even find a way to stop Brown."

"It would be dangerous for you, wouldn't it? Why would you offer this to a stranger?"

Bud lifted a finger and stroked her silky hair. "Lady, I don't mean to push, but I don't intend us to be strangers long."

He'd got the jump on me, but I wasn't going to be left out in the cold. We'd never argued over women, but this one—this time he was going to get a run for his money. I never even thought that the ranch would come with her; it was the girl herself I wanted. She'd hit me between the eyes the minute I'd seen her. I told her, "Miss Livingstone, I've never wanted anything more than I want to ride north with you."

We mounted and rode on. Bud whistled happily, practically purring, his knee all but touching Anne Marie's, and I kept just as close on her other side. I'd always relied a lot on luck and I couldn't remember any as good as this. If we could get Bill Brocious north of the border and separated from his crew we'd have him where we wanted him, in enough jeopardy to get out of him the name of the man who killed Doc Danby and his cooperation in proving Rob Stewart had not.

I had seen a lot of ranches but never one to compare with the Flying L. All of the old Spanish spreads maintained a complete community—

the family hacienda, a store and housing for the Mexicans required to work the place, gardens, orchards, and of course the omnipresent church. The Livingstone layout was the biggest I'd ever come across. It crouched in a wide valley beside a fast-running river, acres of green grain fields around it in sharp contrast to the dusty land we had ridden through. Orchards hid the buildings until we broke through them on the wagon trail; then we saw barns, corrals, a cluster of small adobe houses brightened by red geraniums against the walls, strings of red chilis hanging from the protruding roof poles, and clumps of the thick, grey-green oval-leaved cactus that was a staple of the diet. There was a large mud barracks for the American riders, with a cookshack beside it and long trestle tables in the shade of great old cottonwoods. We passed a blacksmith shop and a row of American-type open wagon sheds. Everywhere there were people working: Mexicans in wide sombreros in the fields, women with bright skirts pounding clothes on the stones along the river, well-mounted riders circling the herd that was being gathered and held in the rolling pastures.

The squat belfrey of the church and the low sloping red-tile roof of the hacienda were all that showed above the top of the mud wall that enclosed them. The wide gate stood open and three men sat their horses outside it, looking toward the herd as we approached. Two rode away toward it, and the third turned toward the gate, discovered us, and was suddenly very still. He had been sitting loose, his weight leaning on one leg, his shoulders forward and big hands crossed on the high horn of the double-cinched saddle. His back straightened, taut. Beside me the girl tensed too.

I had never more than nodded to Curly Bill Brocious but I knew the bulky figure. There was no mistaking that he was alive and prospering here on the Flying L. He put his horse toward us at a slow walk, all his attention on Anne Marie, and when we closed with him he made a show of surprise and concern.

"You home already? Something go wrong in Chihuahua?"

"Not in Chihuahua." The girl's voice was controlled. "Juan came to tell me you were making an early drive. Did you forget I meant to go along?"

He snapped his fingers. "By golly, I sure did. I got worried about drought up the trail—heard it's getting dry already. You leave Juan down south?"

"No," she said steadily. "We were ambushed. He was killed. I would have been if these men hadn't happened by."

He widened his eyes. "Happened by? You mean you tried to travel that road with only Juan? I thought you had better sense. Your aunt will have something to say to you about such a stunt." He looked away from her, first to Bud, then to me, and frowned. "Seems like I ought to know you boys. Seen you somewheres . . ."

"Sam Stewart and Bud Gilbert," I said, and left it there for him to pick up.

He did, sticking out his heavy jaw unpleasantly. "Cactus Kid . . . Yeah. Pals of the Earps."

He made it sound as though we were kin to the devil and I laughed.

"Used to be. They're off the scene now, and we're sort of footloose. Came down to nose around for another game."

Another suspicion narrowed his eyes and he pointed to our saddles. "Where's your gear? You ain't even carrying a canteen."

"We broke camp in a kind of hurry. A gang was shooting at us when we picked up Miss Livingstone. She said she'd send someone to bring the stuff in."

The girl sounded oblivious of the supercharged atmosphere between Brocious and us. "They were looking for a job and when they rescued me I said you would hire them."

That did not delight him either. "You did, huh? You know anything about them? If they can work cattle? They're gamblers, girl, with soft, lily-white hands . . . Where'd you work last, Stewart?"

"Tombstone," I said. "Billy Lee Parks gave me

the faro bank at the Turquoise." I didn't mention the rest of that story, but I got the reaction I wanted. He looked startled.

"You with Billy Lee?"

"Sure. Whitey Bedso brought us in."

It made the difference to him. He relaxed, and we were past the first hurdle. We would not be thrown off the ranch out of hand. I breathed a lot easier, and more so when Brocious said, "Well . . . I guess we can use you for a while. Anne Marie, you go on in and see Carmen, tell her what a crazy thing you tried."

The girl looked at me, a quick glance with a message, and said with sweet guile, "My aunt will want to thank you too, so both of you come to dinner at the house with us." She turned to Brocious with a lift of her head to forestall any challenge that the hired hands dined elsewhere, dismounted and gave her reins to Bud, and went with a leggy stride through the gate.

When she was out of earshot the big outlaw bent a baleful eye on Bud and me, demanding in a flat, hard voice, "You know what my name is?"

I said blandly, "Mike Brown, she told us."

"Don't forget it. And Mister Brown to you. You ever handle cows?" We admitted that we had and he turned his horse in beside us, motioning with a big paw. "Drop the horses at the corral and I'll show you where to bunk. You're going to work your tails off. We got a herd to brand and drive to the border . . . any reason you can't cross the line?"

Bud Gilbert gave him that wide, looping grin. "Might have to shoot a sheriff or two if they get too close."

A sudden, unexpected guffaw broke from Brown—I had to get used to thinking of him by that name—and he sounded more friendly.

"Me and the boys don't let them get close . . . you'll likely know some of the crew riding for me."

We put the horses in the corral, took off the saddles and hung them on a rail, and followed Brown to the big barracks. The bunks lined two sides, three to a tier, seventy-five in all. Added to the Mexican force in their little 'dobes, the ranch apparently used upward of a hundred and fifty men. Brown indicated a middle and upper bunk at the far end of the room as being available, then planted himself spreadlegged before us and told us about the jobs.

"For the branding and the drive you get fifty dollars a month and found . . ."

That was a tipoff in itself, ten dollars higher than the going pay for wranglers.

"After we sell the herd you can stay north or come back here or go where you want. If you come here you'll ride grubline. We don't pay cash except on the drives."

Bud said, "How often do you go?"

"Twice a year."

"Kind of lean pickings in between. What do the men live on?"

Curly Bill screwed his face up in a broad wink. "They make out on their own. This country is full of cattle . . . strays from the ranches the soldiers and bandits have wiped out . . . gone wild . . . lot of young stuff with no brands. We pay eight dollars a head for any that are brought in."

Bud Gilbert whistled softly through his teeth. This had to be one of the biggest rustling operations ever staged. The possibilities were enormous.

Whatever else Mexico was short of it was not cattle. Through the years of revolution the great herds that had once made the hacienda dons among the wealthiest of people had been abandoned as the owners were killed or driven away, and as wild beasts the animals had multiplied profusely. With few ranchers strong enough to survive the raiders, the country teemed with unclaimed stock. Even the Indians in attacking a community wanted only the horses, which they could ride to death and then eat, preferring the meat to beef and not wanting to be encumbered by the dangerous, stubborn longhorned brutes.

Two or three well-equipped and well-mounted men working as a team should be able to gather a couple of hundred head in a week or so. At eight dollars a head the average rider would make much more than even the high wages for the drives. It was no wonder Curly Bill had no trouble recruiting hardcases. The only hazard lay in the possibility of being jumped by roaming bands of Mexican revolutionary bandits.

I gave the outlaw a crooked grin of appreciation. "Mister Brown, I'd say this is an outright gold mine."

"Is if you work at it . . . another thing—you leave anything you want specially back at that camp? I can't afford to send half a dozen men after it. You can outfit at the store here."

There was the photograph of Curly Bill Brocious, but it had served its purpose and I didn't want it to be found among my gear. It would be just as well if the weather bleached the face away. I told him, "If the store stocks some pants and shirts and a deck of cards, that's all we'll need . . . blankets and a slicker and a bandana."

"Uh-huh. You talk Spanish? The storekeeper's a Mex."

We admitted that we did and he pointed out the location of the store and left us.

CHAPTER SEVEN

Cleaned up and decked out in the new clothes, with our hair especially carefully combed for the dinner with Anne Marie, Bud and I caught up our horses and rode the half-mile from the bunkhouse and corral to the hacienda.

It was a big place with thick adobe walls and tile roof fired from the red mud found on the ranch, built like a fortress around a central patio, with the windows facing the yard narrow slits set two feet back in the walls. A squat, fat, moon-faced, barefoot Indian servant girl took us through the main hall, which had been built as a ballroom, and out to the patio. This was a large garden with quince, peach, orange, pomegranate and bananas, the area being one of the few in the province where that fruit ripened. The family lived and ate in the shade of the trees except when it rained, using the house mainly to sleep in, and there had been little dancing in the ballroom since the fall of the Emperor.

The table was round, English oak, set with Spanish linen and silver. Anne Marie, Curly Bill, and a handsome, small black-haired woman in her early thirties were already gathered for the meal. She looked to me too much like Spanish aristocracy to have married Brocious for any reason, except that her dark eyes had a hard calculation and the boldness of a dominator. They would make a hard team to beat, I thought, and maybe Curly Bill had met his match in his wife.

Anne Marie introduced us to her aunt, who thanked us for the rescue of her niece with an effusiveness that was convincingly sincere. Considering what the girl had accused her of doing, I was confused, and even Brocious watched her with startled eyes.

"The dear girl is so rash, so foolishly impulsive," she told us. "She would have got herself killed out there without your help. We would all have suffered a terrible loss."

Anne Marie looked straight at Brocious, her chin lifted. "Yes, you would have, both of you. Aunt Carmen may not have thought to tell you, but she does not inherit from me. My father's will specifies that if I die unmarried Aunt Carmen should be given one quarter of the land, but the hacienda and all the rest will go to his nephew in England."

Curly Bill growled at her. "She told me, all right, and that ain't what she meant about a loss. She's talking about losing her sister's only child and you might show a little gratitude to her."

So I could have been wrong in suspecting the big outlaw of trying to murder Anne Marie, but again, even a quarter of the Flying L was a sizable prize as a base for his rustling. I just did not know where the truth lay. One thing, though, was becoming obvious. Brocious showed an uncharacteristic subdued deference to his wife, and I guessed that Carmen Brown was the stronger force. It was likely to be her imagination that was responsible for the scope of their operations.

Through the dinner Bud Gilbert played up to Anne Marie, and I didn't like the way she responded, bright-eyed and laughing as if she was in no trouble at all. I wanted to do the same, to make her laugh for me, but at the moment it was important for me to convince the aunt that we were no threat to her and her husband, and the charm act kept me busy.

The woman gave me her whole attention, her back turned on her husband as though he had angered her. Brocious sulked, paying no attention to any of us, stuffing himself the way he would stoke a furnace with beef, mountain quail, turkey, beans, and corn bread, swilling it down with Mexican beer. Carmen let one scornful glance at him escape her as he finished, belched, and shoved to his feet saying he had to go give their orders to the night riders who would guard the herd.

After coffee—thick, black, too sweet—Anne Marie got up, saying, "Would you like to see the house?"

It was more a command than an invitation, and

we excused ourselves to the aunt, who made no move to leave the table. The girl linked her hands through both Bud's and my arms and took us on the tour.

"It was built over a hundred years ago," she said. "My father added a wing at the south side for an office and library and I use that now, to keep away from Mike Brown. It has a strong door and lock."

Bud stopped, bristling. "He bothers you?"

The corner of her mouth turned up in irony. "Not too much. He's afraid of Aunt Carmen, but twice when she was away he got drunk and tried to break in. I put a couple of bullets through the door and he went away and didn't try again."

I couldn't help laughing at the picture of the big brute being run off by this fragile-looking girl, but Bud didn't see it as funny.

"Somebody ought to break his head," he growled. "Why Wyatt missed . . ."

I coughed and he cut it off short, but the girl looked sharply at each of us. "You know something that I don't?"

Bud was usually an artful liar but this time he said weakly, "I mean Marshal Earp cleaned out most of the border toughs but somehow he missed your precious uncle. Your aunt must want money mighty bad to put up with him."

Her voice dripped acid. "It isn't exactly a love match and they don't even trust each other. Did you notice when I explained about the will how mad she got? She thinks Mike tried to have me killed behind her back. And maybe if she got some of the property he'd kill her for that. Funny, isn't it, that I have to depend on her for my safety while she tries to steal enough of the cattle money to force me to sell her the ranch."

"Funny ha-ha," Bud told her. "And I'm going to see that doesn't go on."

When we left and headed for the bunkhouse he continued grumbling. "The old witch. Laura Whitaker made a mistake marrying Doc Danby instead of your dad, but this one . . . taking on an animal like Brocious . . . I'm going to stop them cold."

"I? Not we?"

He gave me a sudden wide grin. "Oh, you can play too, but I'm going to marry Anne Marie."

"Maybe . . . maybe not. You're going to have some competition, and I'll bet you she prefers me."

Bud swung toward me, his jaw dropping. "You . . . ? You keep out of it."

I said, "I saw her first. I've got prior claim."

"By three seconds." He sounded hot under the collar. "And I'm in love with her."

"Afraid I am too, old buddy. Every man for himself and I'll do my damnedest to beat your time."

"You'll have to get up early and stay up late," he said, then was silent as we rode the lane. We were almost at the corral when he heaved a sigh, sounding unhappy. "When she takes me is it going to break us up?"

"How about it the other way around?"

Neither of us had found an answer by the time we walked through the bunkhouse door; then the dismal prospect of a woman coming between us was out the window for a while.

We had each bought two pair of trousers and a couple of shirts with the other duffel from the ranch store, using part of the thousand dollars Bud had borrowed from his old man so we could get out of Tombstone. Now all the gear, new and old, lay scattered across the floor at the rear of the bunkhouse, behind the three poker tables strung down the long room.

There were six men at each table, others kibitzing, and a few reading *Police Gazettes* on the bunks. Not a one of them glanced toward the door as Bud went through it and stopped so short that I bumped into him. I had one glimpse of blankets and pants-legs tied in tight knots and of a shirt ripped up the back to the collar, then I had other things to keep track of. We had expected some sort of rawhiding—there always was when a new man joined an outfit, and Bud had taken on more than one crew bully before we had been accepted—but we had not yet even met these men, and with the girl on our minds the vandalism came as a shock.

Bud spoke in a toneless voice that carried to the corners of the room: "Will the yellow son of a bitch who had this bright idea speak up, or do I have to lick the lot of you?"

A man at the farthest poker table came to his feet, slow, his hips weaving—a gorilla, not very tall but built like a barrel, with thick legs and arms too long for the rest of him. His heavy mouth widened and he licked his lips, smacked them, looking toward eating Bud Gilbert whole. His voice was like a club.

"Sonny boy been eating raw meat or does he think the lady boss will come slap my wrist?"

Bud began a slow prowl toward him. The men on the bunks sat up and the people around the tables moved quickly, hauling the furniture out of the way, then started to circle in behind Bud. I stayed by the door, my gun in my hand, and called out:

"Keep back, all of you."

They swung around, saw the gun, and stopped moving. The gorilla laughed and flapped a hand at me. "Put it away, we're just going to have a little fun with your friend; then you can have what's left of him. I'm going to take him apart."

"Go ahead and try. I just want it understood that it's a two-man show. Any of the rest of you get an idea of mixing in—don't."

Three of them looked as if they would go for their guns, but another said sharply, "That's the Cactus Kid... Watch out."

The three spread their hands, moved them away from the holsters, and everyone backed to the walls, watching me until the fight began.

It started slowly, the big man coming to meet Bud in a crouch, the long arms hanging forward, the powerful hands splayed for grabbing. Then Bud jumped, threw a left against the jaw and a right that jarred the big head. The gorilla ignored both, making a quick grab for Bud's shoulders, but Bud was fast, dancing back, planting himself and throwing fists. The room was perfectly quiet except for the smack of his blows connecting. They had no apparent effect on the bully. He weaved forward with wide spaced steps, maneuvering Bud toward the bunks, where he would have no room for further backing.

Men moved aside, clearing the way, and one said in a tight voice, "Come on, Lemon... Take him."

One of Bud's legs touched the bunk frame. He raised the foot against it and pushed for extra thrust, lunged in and swung three short, hard punches under Lemon's heart as the gorilla tried to wrap his arms around Bud's waist. Lemon's breath rushed out, but he fell against Bud and his hands clamped together at Bud's spine. Big as Gilbert was, the man could snap his back with a grip like that. Bud did not give him the time. He pivoted to face the bunk, turning in Lemon's arms, doubled over, dropped his head near the floor and rammed Lemon over his back onto the wooden frame. The bully scrambled up, shook his head groggily, but came on again, still reaching. Bud jammed a knee into the groin and, when Lemon's hands clamped down against the pain, used his shoulder to butt the big head back. He stepped away then and almost casually measured the man, crashed a right to the jaw, then a left, then drove the right between the man's eyes, opening a deep cut in one eyebrow.

Lemon staggered back and Bud was on him like a cat, slicing the heavy face to ribbons. The long arms no longer reached for a victim, they were wrapped around the head, trying to protect it from the onslaught. He doubled down to his knees, to his hands. Instinct stronger than reason made him grab the edge of the bunk and haul himself up, fighting to keep his feet.

Bud stepped back, dropped his arms to his sides, and said in a flat voice, "Had enough?"

The gorilla appeared not to hear. He lowered his head, stretched out his arms like feelers, and blindly stumbled forward to fight on. Bud waited until he was almost within reach, then brought a fist up from his boot top, swung all his weight to his shoulder to slash against the bent head.

The man went over backward, turning, landed

on his face, sprawled on the floor and lay without moving. Bud blew on his bleeding knuckles, the only marks on him, turned to look over the watching crew, not even short of breath, and said quietly, "Next."

Silence answered him, a stunned, unbelieving silence. Bud chose a man nearly as big as Lemon and pointed to the rear of the room.

"Untie those blankets and clothes and make up the bunks."

The man shook his head quickly, stepping back. "I didn't tie them—"

"Move—or point out who did it."

The man stood a moment longer, swallowed, his Adam's apple running up and down, then went to the scattered gear and crouched over it, working at the knots. No one else in the room moved. No one made a sound. Then there was a scrape of boots in the yard and I stepped aside to cover the door. Curly Bill came into the rectangle of light and stopped in the entrance.

His dark eyes took in the unconscious Lemon, the man in the middle of the litter, and Bud Gilbert, now sucking at his knuckles. He looked over the crew with a puzzled expression, then discovered me and the gun in my hand. One corner of his mouth curved down.

"Put it up."

I put it up.

Brocious flapped a hand at Lemon and said to

the room in general, "Haul him out and throw some water on him."

Two men jumped for Lemon's feet and dragged him into the yard, left him lying in the light, and went for buckets. It took three dousings before the gorilla stirred, groaned, and gathered himself to sit up.

Brocious stood over him, sounding disgusted. "See you finally tackled somebody who could whale the hell out of you. You've had it coming a long time."

Lemon looked up through eyes swollen to slits, his bloody face bewildered. Curly Bill turned his back to the room, his voice loud.

"Hit the sack. I want that herd branded and ready to move in three days." He came around to face me squarely. "And you—don't be so quick to pull that hogleg on my boys. There are some in here who can take it away from you and make you eat it." He raised his voice again. "If I see a light in here in ten minutes I'll shoot it out and I don't really care who I hit."

CHAPTER EIGHT

There is no work on earth hotter than that of branding in midsummer in Chihuahua. The fire was laid in a long slit trench a foot deep and kept fed by half-grown Mexican kids. Other youngsters had the job of seeing that the irons tossed aside by the branding crew were put back in the coals, carefully so the handles would not get hot.

After Bud's handling of Lemon we worked in moderate harmony with the others. Wranglers cut animals out of the holding herd, drove them to the trench, and threw them. The big brutes were held down while the line of men at the fire ran the road brand on the flanks, then they were kicked up and hazed in among the bellowing, milling animals ready for travel. Besides the Flying L there were several other brands, some old, on stock gone wild, some fresher, on cattle from three neighbor ranches to be added into our drive.

The air was choking with the stench of burning hair and hide and a cloud of churned dust so thick we could not see the team next to us. We worked all morning at a half run, with hardly time to toss aside a cooling iron and catch up a hot one before the next steer was dumped in front of us.

We ate a noon meal in shifts, fresh men taking over while we mopped sweat and mud off our hands and faces, spent fifteen minutes at the table and half an hour sprawled in the blistering shade, then we were back at the trench for the afternoon. I had worked herds before, but more of my time had been spent at a gaming table and I was not as hardened to this as the regular crew. Never in my life had I put in a day like that first one. By the time Curly Bill called a halt, sweat blinded me and my clothes were soggy with wet mud, and I ached in every muscle.

I beckoned to Bud and headed for the clear, cold river across the meadow, telling him, "I am going to jump in there just as I am."

"Better take off your gun. I'll race you."

Bigger, longer-legged than I, he reached the bank first, dropping his belt and thrashing into the waist-deep current. I was right behind, throwing myself in a shallow dive, going under, floating there, letting the water buoy me to the surface, simply hanging limp while the cold soaked through me, soaked out the tiredness. When I felt that I could move I kicked to the bank, stripped and scrubbed what mud I could out of my clothes, climbed out and spread them over a bush, then dropped full length in the deep grass. Bud left his wet clothes on and stretched out and we both slept. By the time we waked up the hot Mexican sun had dried both our outfits, and when I had dressed we started toward the bunkhouse.

Inside, the crew sagged in the chairs around the tables or sprawled in the bunks. The big bully Lemon sat leaning forward, arms across his knees, looking all in, battered from Bud's beating and worn out by the day's labor on top of it. Bud veered toward him as soon as he was through the door, sticking out his hand.

"Quits?"

Lemon squinted up and touched tenderly at his bruised mouth. "Quits. I know when I've been licked." The words came slurred through lips still partly paralyzed.

Bud went on to his bunk, dug under the mattress for the tequila bottle he'd got at the store, took it back and extended it silently to Lemon. The man's eyes widened; he took the bottle and drank deeply, making a face as the fiery liquor burned the cuts in his mouth and started tears in his eyes. He handed the bottle back and Bud drank, did not offer it to me, but jammed the cork tight and tossed it casually onto his bunk, then looked at the watching crew, his eyes daring anyone to touch it.

Washed without soap, my clothes still stank and I went to change to the other set and use a comb. There was just a chance that sometime between now and night Anne Marie might show up. Bud gave me a sly grin, changed too, then went out to the yard and sat on a bench in the late sun, watching the hacienda gate like a cat at a mousehole. For myself, I'd had enough sun for the day, and my hands were stiff, sore, so I stayed inside at an empty table, working with a deck of cards to keep them flexible.

Lemon got up and walked out. Through the door I saw him sit down unasked beside Bud, and they talked until the cook's triangle rang the call to supper. The crew tumbled out, hunger shown in their hurry. I waited until the room was empty, had a drink from my own bottle, then started for the cookshack and the eating hall beside it. Lemon had moved with the crew and Bud stood up, waiting for me. We walked without hurry, lagging out of earshot.

"He's not a bad sort now he knows how he stands," Bud said. "I got talking to him about the drive, got some dope. We take the herd just south of the border and turn it over to a crew Billy Lee Parks sends down. None of us goes over the line. So when do we spring our gold shipment on Brocious to get him across?"

I told him, "I don't think that will work now I've seen what he's got here. We couldn't invent a transfer big enough to tempt him to risk going after it while he can make all he wants out of this ranch and the rustling."

"I don't know . . ." Bud wasn't convinced. "He's a greedy cuss and he's not afraid of God or the devil. Look at the way he and the McLowerys used to thumb their nose at the law up north."

"Sure. Before that federal warrant was put out for him. It's one thing to do business with the Tucson Ring and something else to take a chance on being spotted by some marshal when everybody believes he's dead. I think we'll have to play along and watch for another way to nail him. If we survive this branding chore."

Bud laughed at me. "Got you down, has it? You'd better survive. You've got your dad to get out of Yuma and I sure don't want Curly Bill for an uncle-in-law."

"You needn't worry," I said. "Anne Marie will marry me as soon as I get rid of him for her."

The crew was already at the table when we got there, barely leaving room on one long bench for the pair of us, and the cook with two helpers was dealing out platters piled high with beef and corn cakes, vats of fiery hot beans. There was little table talk, the hungry men too busy stowing away food and too tired to waste energy on conversation.

When we were finished we all drifted back to the bunkhouse and the inevitable poker games got under way. Bud nodded at an empty chair.

"Now's a good time to start making up that thousand for my dad and getting us a stake. We aren't going to collect any wages until the end of the drive." He added under his breath, "And

I don't suppose we will then." Aloud he told me, "Why don't you sit in?"

"What are you going to do?"

"Look on awhile."

His while didn't last long. The first hand had been dealt and the first round of bets made when he stepped from behind my chair, said, "Guess I'll go watch the sunset," and sauntered out to the yard. There wasn't a thing I could do but let him go and just hope he did not find Anne Marie.

I won steadily for an hour, but it was cold comfort to think of the old adage: lucky at cards, unlucky in love. And I couldn't get away. If I was going to go with the herd to the border I didn't want a chip on the shoulder of any of these hardcases because I walked out of a game early and a heavy winner. A man called Pete was dealing and I caught a third king to my opening pair. Slim, on my right, called and raised. He had drawn only one card. If he helped with a straight or flush he had me beat, but if he held only two pair and had not filled my threes were good.

Curly Bill Brocious came in, looked over the room, then walked to my table and stood quietly while I won the pot. As I drew the money in he said, "See you outside a minute, Stewart."

I nodded and started to get up, but Slim yelped. "Hell, Mike, the guy's way ahead. Don't pull him out now."

Brocious gave him a sour grunt, said, "Might

save you some dough," and jerked his head toward the door.

I stacked my winnings in front of me and said to the table as a whole, "Take care of it until I get back," and followed the foreman out.

Curly Bill crossed the yard, not stopping until he reached the corral; then he faced around, his thumb hitched in his belt very close to the butt of his revolver, his heavy jaw thrust forward in a challenge and his voice flat with threat.

"I've been thinking all day, Kid. I recognized you when you rode in, right off. Did you recognize me?"

Whatever he had been thinking, the worst thing I could do would be to deny I knew him, but I couldn't guess what his reaction would be. I made my smile easy, my voice careless as though his identity was no concern of mine.

"Sure I did. You're Curly Bill Brocious. I used to see you around Tombstone. Why?"

The black eyes probed at me in the afterlight of the day, suspicious. "Did it surprise you to see me?"

I lifted my shoulders, trying to figure where the danger here lay. "Sort of. When you disappeared the *Nugget* ran a story that you were alive, but the *Epitaph* claimed you were dead. And there was the grave that Wyatt sent back word was yours."

"Earp. Yeah. And you sided with them."

"While he was marshal I did. As a gambler I liked the odds better where the star was. We weren't friends; I beat that crazy Holliday in too many games for that."

"Maybe." His suspicion didn't ease, it grew. "And maybe you came down here looking for me."

This was delicate ground. I had to throw him off that track or there'd be a fight. I wasn't afraid of him, not in the sense that I thought he could kill me. I knew how good I was with a gun. But I didn't want to have to kill him. Alive, he might help me clear my father, but dead, he would be worse than useless because he was the only link I had with Danby's murderer. I showed him a puzzled face.

"How do you think I'd have known where to find you?"

"You could have found out in Chihuahua. You could have come to this ranch deliberately because you knew I was here. Did you?"

"What reason would I have? I never knew you up north."

His voice hammered at me. "The Earps sent you."

My mouth opened in genuine surprise, then I laughed aloud. "Don't you know enough about Earp to know that if he learned you were here and wanted you dead he'd come after you himself? He wouldn't send anybody. That isn't his way."

That backed him up a little and he stood undecided, thinking it over, then slowly nodded; but he wasn't ready to buy my story and changed his charge against me.

"Maybe you came to try to blackmail me on your own."

"Blackmail? Me? For God's sake, have I said anything to give you that idea? You think I'm stupid enough to come in where you've got fifty guns and threaten you? I'd be dead before I could blink."

It took effort to control my sudden excitement that I seemed to have guessed right, and his next words confirmed it.

"It was tried," he said tightly. "A man discovered a picture of me I had taken after I was supposed to be dead. He got word to some friends of mine that he'd forget it for five thousand dollars. He got a bullet in his back instead."

"Not surprising," I said. "I don't know anything about it."

"Somebody does. The picture wasn't found on his body. Somebody got it. Maybe you."

"If I'd been the blackmailer I sure wouldn't carry the thing around on me. I'd have hid it for life insurance. What does it matter anyway?"

"They want me north of the line. If it gets out I'm alive . . ."

I used a careless shrug and laugh. "I'd say most of the men on this ranch are wanted somewhere up there. I wouldn't let it bother me down here." This time he showed a hesitation and I added, "I've got enough trouble up there of my own without hunting more with you, but if my being on the ranch worries you I'll move on."

"No . . ." he said it slowly. "I guess you're in the clear, and I can use every hand I can dig up. I watched you and Gilbert today. You do all right. I need a crew big enough to drive ten thousand steers without losing a lot to herd jumpers, and still have men enough to leave to protect the ranch. If I didn't the damned Mexican deserters would swarm over the place before we were half a day up the trail."

It came as a jolt to think Brocious might mean to leave Bud and me as part of the guard, but I didn't dare mention it. Then he took me off that hook, saying, "We'll start Monday or Tuesday of next week if the branding is finished. You and Gilbert get what you need for the drive from the store."

So another jump was cleared and his suspicion was replaced by an abrupt heartiness, a heavy chuckle. "Get on back to your game now, and if you're as good with cards as I heard you'll have every peso in the crew before we start north."

He stepped around me and without once looking back strode to the hacienda and went through the gate. I stayed where I was, working the tension out from between my shoulders, breathing slowly to bring back relaxation, only now realizing how strung up the duel with Brocious had made me.

CHAPTER NINE

I was still standing by the corral when movement down near the river made me look that way. It was not yet full dark and I made out two figures, one big and the other slight, small. Bud Gilbert and Anne Marie, I was sure. I did not go back to the poker game. Money isn't all there is to living. I walked down to intercept them and got a chilly welcome from Bud.

"What's the matter?" he growled. "The game break you?"

"You know better," I told him. "I'm over a thousand ahead, enough to pay off your dad and keep us going tomorrow. I've had enough for tonight."

"That's not very smart, Kid. Those hombres aren't going to like your pulling out with that much money, and we've got a ways to ride with them. You'd better get on back and do your job."

I had fallen in on the other side of the girl and was talking across her head. "Later maybe. I've got some news. I just had a talk with Curly Bill . . ."

It was out before I could stop it and this time Anne Marie caught me up on the name.

"With who?"

"Mike Brown." There was no way to avoid

telling her, now that I'd made the slip. If I tried to evade it she'd probably ask someone else and land in more trouble than she already had. "It's a nickname he had up north. But don't ever call him that, don't ever say it to anyone."

She kept looking at me, puzzled and disturbed. "There's something important about the nickname, isn't there? Something dangerous? I know he's an outlaw, but what is it I don't know?"

I shook my head, my brain suddenly too numb to think of any answer I wanted to give her, and she twisted her head to Bud Gilbert and demanded, "You tell me then. I want to know what's going on. Who are you siding with? My uncle?"

Bud craned his neck around as if his collar was too tight and threw me a cornered look, dropped his eyes and said unhappily, "It's Sam's game, not mine. Up to him to tell you if he thinks he ought to."

She swung away from him, planted herself in front of me solidly and tilted her chin up in defiance.

"Well, Mr. Sam Stewart? I am waiting."

I didn't like it a bit. There was no telling how she would react to the story, but now that she was suspicious of us, thought that maybe we'd thrown in with her uncle and aunt, I decided I had better tell her at least part of the truth, warn her about letting Brocious get any inkling that she knew we were interested in him. I tried to sound casual.

"It's just that your uncle's name isn't Mike Brown. It's Bill Brocious, Curly Bill Brocious, and in the states he was head of one of the worst gangs of cutthroats Arizona ever suffered."

She was impatient. "I know he's an outlaw. They're the only kind of Americans who come down here in numbers enough to keep the bandits from overrunning us. And he's a leader type, so it's reasonable that he'd be the boss up north of men like . . ."

Her words trailed off in embarrassment as she remembered that Bud and I were below the line and she knew nothing about us, that we were probably outlaws ourselves; then she plowed ahead with that imperiousness we'd seen before.

"But that isn't all of it. There's something more, I know, and I'm going to find out what it is. If you won't tell me I'll ask him myself."

Bud Gilbert caught both her shoulders and whirled her around, bending to put his face almost against hers. "Honey," he said urgently, "don't do a thing like that . . . Please . . . You'll get yourself killed for sure." He looked past her at me, his face furious. "You get her out of this, Kid, or you and I are going to tangle—right now."

"All right," I told her sickly, "I'll tell you. We didn't just happen down here by accident. We knew Brocious was at the ranch and were on our way here to get him."

She had twisted out of Bud's hands and again had me pinned with her eyes, saying, "Go on. Why? Are you bounty hunters or law officers or what?"

There just wasn't any way left but to tell her the whole thing. We were standing close to a fallen cottonwood and I went over to sit down on it, beckoning to the girl. She sat down beside me and Bud stood over us, his fists knotted, ready to throw them at me unless I satisfied her completely. I began at the beginning, when Bud and I rode into Silver and learned about my father, and told her every move we had made since, and why.

"So you see," I finished, "my only chance of getting Rob Stewart out of Yuma is to prove who really killed Doc Danby, and Bill Brocious has to be the key, he has to have ordered the murder. And"—I looked up at Bud—"while I was talking to Bill a few minutes ago he accused me of coming here to blackmail him. He said it had already been tried, that a man had found a photograph of him taken after Earp was reported to have killed him, and wanted five thousand dollars for it."

Bud whistled softly through his teeth and looked mollified. Anne Marie was quiet, believing me but puzzling over what would come next. Finally she said, "Do you really think a man like Mike . . . Brocious would help you by implicating himself? I think he'd laugh at you if you asked."

"Sure he would if we just asked," Bud took over. "What we have to do is sucker him into crossing the border. There's a federal warrant for his arrest up there. We want to capture him, then make a trade, let him go in return for proof of who killed Danby."

She came to her feet violently, in protest, her voice scornful and outraged. "You would do a thing like that to me? After you said you'd look out for my interests?"

We both gaped at her. I know I didn't and I thought Bud didn't have the least idea of what she meant. She looked from one to the other, then added, spacing out her words, "While you have that man away from his cutthroat crew, what do you think will become of the money paid for the cattle?"

"Oh."

It was a bolt of lightning, an angle I hadn't even considered, and while I tried to fit it into some plan she went on, rubbing in her meaning.

"Have you any idea what that herd will bring? Almost two hundred thousand dollars. American. About half of that is mine. Some of it is due our three neighbors who pay us to drive their animals with ours. It is paid in Mexico. In cash. If you take Brocious above the line even for a day the money will vanish. I don't like him or trust him, and I know he steals from me, but as long as he is present to control the crew the men are afraid of him and not one of them would dare lay a finger on the money. But if you snatch him away what becomes of the ranch? What becomes of me?"

I didn't say anything because I hadn't any answer to give her. I'd have to do a lot of thinking to find one. But she didn't give me the time then. She turned her back on us and walked rapidly toward the house.

Bud called after her, "Wait for me, Anne Marie, I'll see you home."

Her voice came back over her shoulder, the coldest I had heard it yet. "Thank you, no. I have walked this meadow many times at night and been safer than I am with either of you."

We watched her go, two big, smart, capable males routed by this slip of a girl. Bud swore at me in two languages. "That tears it. You and your fat mouth. What will she do now?"

I was feeling down enough without being told and my tone showed it. "I'd say the natural thing would be for her to go up there and warn her aunt and Bill what we had in mind . . . and next there'll be a couple of ropes tossed over a branch and us jumping at the ends. If we had any sense we'd hit the corral now, saddle up, and hightail out of here pronto. Matter of fact, you'd better do just that."

"Me, huh? Why just me?"

"Why get your neck broken? It isn't your dad in prison. If I run I'll never get this close to Brocious again."

"And if she tells him you'll never get him within two days of the line. Besides, you don't expect me to ride out and leave her to his tender mercies, do you?"

I was between the devil and the deep sea. If we stayed and she warned Brocious, we were dead men, and dead men wouldn't be much protection for her. I said it aloud. Bud kicked at the dust and shook his head.

"I'm willing to bet she doesn't open her mouth up there. I don't think she wants to see us hung and she's smart enough to have figured out by now that if Bill hears she knows about him her own chances wouldn't be so good."

"Well . . . maybe . . . but maybe she's too mad about the money to think . . . What do you say we ought to do?"

"Go back to the bunkhouse and get in the poker game and hang onto the idea that she credits us with saving her life. I'll take the chance if you will."

I got off the log and started walking. "So who's the gambler? Let's go."

CHAPTER TEN

We did not go directly to the bunkhouse. We went to the corral and saddled five horses, took two up beside the hacienda gate and tied them there, and hitched the others in the dark at the side of the bunkhouse. Bud didn't come in and join the game but sat outside, watching. We figured if the girl talked to Brocious he would come ramming down himself. With most of his men in the room he wouldn't be worried about taking the two of us—but before he could reach the door Bud could lay a gun barrel over his head, whistle for me, and I could walk quietly out. We could tie Bill on one horse, ride up to the house and get the two women for hostage, and be away from the ranch before anything was discovered.

I sat in the game for an hour but my luck for the night had run out. Luck doesn't stay with a player whose mind isn't wholly on the cards, and mine wasn't. I kept listening for a bird call. I lost back half of what I'd won earlier and the only thing good about it was that the men at my table were happier at my losing than they had been when I was so far ahead. Lemon was heavy winner now and in a mood unusually good for him when the door opened and a tall, smooth-faced young Mexican stepped through and looked over the room.

"Hey, Spik," Lemon hailed him. "What you doing here, looking for a game?"

The man smiled, a white flash of teeth, shook his head and came over to me. "Señor Brown," he said, "says the new men should come quickly to the hacienda."

The deal was just beginning. I put what money I had left in my pocket, stood up and settled my gun belt, and walked out behind the Mexican. If it was an ambush I wanted him in front of me.

No shot came. The messenger got on his horse and rode off and I went on to where Bud was invisible in the heavy shadow of a tree.

"You guessed wrong, Bud," I said. "She must have told him. Brocious sent for us. To come to the house. I wonder what that means."

Bud stood up without hurry. "One way to find out."

"Walk into a firing squad? Last chance to hit the trail. You—"

"I," he said, "am not going anywhere and leaving that girl here. If I can't get her clear I'll get shot trying."

Both of us spun as someone moved out of another shadow and our guns were in our hands before we recognized the figure that ran toward us. It was Anne Marie. I looked beyond for Brocious but there was no sign of anyone else; then the girl was with us, whispering urgently.

"Now I am in trouble. Now I need help in a hurry."

Bud caught her and held her against him, tipping her chin up with a finger. "Brocious?"

"Both of them. We had an argument and they locked me in my room."

"You told him about Sam and me?"

"No. I was going to, but when I calmed down a little I knew he would kill you and probably me too. But I didn't intend to let you take him north of the line and let the money be stolen. Then I thought, I could take my vaqueros on the drive to protect it until Brocious came back."

I interrupted her. "I haven't seen any vaqueros. Where are they?"

"In the Mexican community. Some of the families have lived here for generations. They worked for my mother's people. My father didn't think they were capable of handling the raiders but he let them stay on the ranch, grow peppers and beans and raise goats, even let them take an occasional beef, but when Mike Brown took over he wouldn't even let them work the cattle at all. They're loyal to me, though."

Loyal they might be, and a working vaquero is a man to be respected—he can be as tough as any hardcase and he is noted for taking lightly the life of an enemy. But by the girl's report these Mexicans were a generation away from the kind of raiders that could equal Brocious's outlaws with guns or knives, young men who had been raised in peace on these acres, with no responsibility given to them. I didn't have much faith in their protecting anything on a cattle drive.

Anne Marie was telling us the rest of her predicament. "At the house I found Carmen and Mike in the room he uses as an office, going over tally sheets. I asked him when we would be starting north and my aunt jumped on the word *we*. Apparently my uncle had not told her I was going on the drive, and she went through the ceiling, stormed around that a girl unescorted could not ride with the men, so I told her she ought to come along."

Bud Gilbert chuckled. "I'll bet that went over strong."

"Oh, it did. You should have heard her: 'ME? Go on a cattle drive? What would everybody say?' I asked what everybody she meant and Brown laughed at her and said, 'Yeah, who?' Then she was mad at both of us, snapping that she didn't need his bad jokes and that no niece of hers was going riding through that hostile country with a crew of ruffians, and that was the end of it. I wasn't going to be bullied by her and said it wasn't the end but the beginning, that she couldn't give me orders because I was over twenty-one and the ranch belonged to me, not her."

"Nice," Bud said. "Very neat."

"Not nice enough. Because I was used to my father talking to me as if I had the same rights as a man I had forgotten something. I am only half English. Under Mexican law an unmarried woman has no control over her own property. Her nearest male relative has all the say, and my only blood relative is the one in England who has never been in this country and has no interest in the ranch—he doesn't even write . . .

"Carmen brought it up, said her husband was my uncle by marriage and I was so mad I said law or no law I was taking the vaqueros and going on the drive. That was a big mistake, telling her. She told me to go to my room. I refused and Mike grabbed me and told Carmen to keep me shut up until he came back, and locked me in my bedroom. But I tied the blankets together and climbed down them out the window and went to Pedro Navarro's house."

Bud was stroking her hair, laughing silently, as proud as if she had licked the whole Brocious crew single-handed. "That's my girl . . . Who is Navarro?"

"Major domo of the vaqueros. He's Opata Indian—they were slaves under the Spanish Conquistadores. His family has lived here nearly three hundred years . . . Pedro taught me to ride, he would do anything for me, but I knew when Carmen found I was gone Mike would call out the crew and search the Mexican houses until they found me and hang the people who had helped me. Then I thought of you two. I have to get married. My husband will have legal charge of my property and Brown and Carmen won't have a leg to stand on."

It was a dazzling idea. I caught her hand before Bud could tighten his hold and tugged her to me, wrapped my arms around her.

"I'm mighty pleased to oblige you, Anne Marie . . . but are you sure? You don't know much about either of us."

"I know I'll get a better shake than I have now. And the vaqueros need a male leader. They're brave and they'll fight, but they have to have someone to follow . . . But not you, Sam. You have your father to get out of prison. Bud . . . will you . . . ?"

Gilbert sashayed the two steps between us, took my wrists and pulled my arms open, laughed triumphantly, and stepped back with the girl I loved. "Honey, the only little problem we have now is, where do we get married?"

"In the church. Father Domingo lives right next door. Let's hurry. Carmen might decide to look in my room, and it's a long walk to the hacienda."

"I've got a wedding present for you," Bud said. "Horses right here, all ready."

I did not feel at all like going to a wedding. This wedding. And I was not at all sure there would be one. I said, "The father, won't he be afraid of a reprisal by Brocious? Would he take the risk?"

"He will. He knows how religious Carmen is. She'd kill Mike herself if anything happened to her padre."

There was nothing more I could do to forestall losing the girl. I followed the pair unhappily, watched Bud boost her onto the animal we had saddled for Curly Bill. Then we rode to the wall, left the animals outside and slipped through the dark to the little adobe squatting beside the church.

Anne Marie knocked on the slab door, not loud but a long series of raps. It was a while before a lamp was lighted inside and the door edged open, the priest putting his head out. We stayed out of the rectangle of light while Anne Marie whispered, "Please come outside and close the door, Father. I need you."

Surprise creased the round, well-fed face, and suspicious eyes went beyond the girl to Bud and me. Before he moved he said, "Daughter, what is it? Who are these men?"

"Friends," she said quickly. "Please, either come out or put out the lamp and let us in before we're seen."

The padre chose to blow out the lamp, stand aside while we filed through the door. Then he closed the door and made a new light and looked at the girl, questioning.

She said immediately, "This is Bud Gilbert,

Father. I want you to marry us. I have to get married."

There was sudden shock on the priest's face. The girl saw it and flushed, hurrying on. "It's not what you're thinking . . . It's my aunt and her husband. They're trying to take my ranch, and under our law they can do it unless I have a husband to manage it for me. Isn't that right?"

His full mouth made a round O and his breath came out in a long sigh. He looked Bud over from the crown of his head to his boot soles with anything but friendliness, then put his anxious eyes on the girl.

"Child, you know how dear you are to me and that I would do anything in my power for you, if it were right. But this . . . this is jumping out of the pan into the fire. As your husband, this man whom I do not know would have all power over you. I do not know how he would use it."

"I'd use it to keep her property from being stolen from her," Bud said promptly.

"Anne Marie." The priest ignored Bud. "What makes you believe him? He is American. North American. From what we both know of the breed, how can you trust him? How long have you known him?"

He was perfectly right, and I would have preferred a long courtship and a much different outcome, but Bud didn't appreciate being compared to Brocious's gang and his voice roughened.

"It doesn't matter how long she's known me. I love her. I wanted her even before I knew who she is and I'll do the best I can for her. What more can any man promise?"

It made me sick to see the girl's eyes, all at once glowing with confidence, with happiness. It might begin as a match of convenience but it wasn't going to stay simply that for long. The priest saw it too, and the way Bud's eyes matched hers. His lips prayed silently, then with another sigh he took her hand and led her through the door connecting his house with the church.

Bud kept close behind them and I trailed further back. The padre lit his candles and picked up his book and performed the service, keeping it short, to finish before there should be an interruption. I watched it through until Bud Gilbert took his new wife in his arms with sober ceremony. Then I wanted to turn away, but I could not. I too had to kiss the bride.

CHAPTER ELEVEN

I knew there would be fireworks from Carmen and Bill Brocious. When we left the church I said, "Shall we roust them out of bed and tell them, or wait for morning?"

Bud had one of her small hands tucked possessively under his arm and she reached the other for me just the way she had done before she made her vows. It wasn't easy, letting her touch me now.

"They won't be in bed," she said. "I don't know how Mike keeps going on as little sleep as he gets. They play head-and-head poker most of the night."

Bud had a quiet laugh. "Curly Bill feathering his nest with every angle he can think of?"

A little gaiety came through her tension in an answering laugh. "Not with cards. He taught her to play and she beats him almost every game. But they don't play for real money, only credit. He owes her over a million dollars by now."

We went through the house quietly and saw light under the office door and pushed it open. I went first because I'm faster with a gun than Bud and he had a fresh responsibility to stay alive.

Brocious hit his feet, his big hand slapping toward his holster, almost turning over the table they were playing on. Then he saw that I had him covered and stood very still. I said, "Relax, Mike. We thought you two might like to help the kids celebrate."

His murderous eyes shot to his wife, then to Bud with his left arm around the girl and his right splayed close to his gun butt, and last he looked at the radiant Anne Marie. I think he knew instinctively what she had done, but he said anyway, "Celebrate what?"

Anne Marie beat both of us with the answer. "My wedding. Mike . . . Aunt Carmen, I am Mrs. Bud Gilbert. Father Domingo just married us and registered it in the records."

There wasn't a sound or a movement for a long moment, then Carmen stood up, steadying herself with a hand on the table and shook a long, blue-veined finger at the girl, but her voice wasn't aristocracy. She sounded like a screech owl.

"You . . . You . . . You've barely met this . . . this vagabond. You've done this deliberately, to get rid of me. I, who have watched over and kept you safe from the ruffians we must hire."

Anne Marie smiled, calm and composed. "Deliberately, yes. Not to get rid of you, dear aunt, but to claim my ranch."

The older woman shrieked. "Why you ungrateful English tart." She jumped for the girl, her clawed hands outstretched to choke her.

"That's enough." Bud moved in front of his

bride, caught Carmen's wrists, spun her and threw her at Curly Bill.

Bill's reaction was muscle reflex. He caught the stumbling woman and held her while she found her balance.

Bud said in a flat voice, "You make her behave or I will. Take your choice."

Brocious's choice was in his flaming eyes. He wanted to blow Bud's head off, but he was an old hand at knowing how to act when he was under a gun. He whispered something under his voice to his wife, savagely, and pushed her into the chair, then said aloud, "Shut up now. Let's see what we've got here. Gilbert, you're pretty slick, aren't you? You going to try to throw me out and take the herd north yourself?"

Bud gave him a lazy, easy smile and tightened his arm around the girl's shoulder. "Hadn't thought to, Mike. Billy Lee Parks might not like your losing clear out. If you say so we can work together fine."

Brocious stood there, a great brute bulk, peering steadily at Bud; then without warning he threw his head back and guffawed.

"Hell now, man, maybe this ain't going to be too bad after all. Sure, Gilbert. Sure. I'll throw in with you. There's plenty for everybody."

He came forward, moving cautiously, wary of me, and thrust out a horny paw. Bud didn't take it right away. He said, "We get one thing straight. The ranch belongs to my wife and I give the orders. You're foreman until I catch you undercutting us. Do that and you're out."

Curly Bill's heavy, cruel mouth stretched in a red grin. "You're on, boy."

Bud took the hand then for a brief shake.

Carmen had not said another word. Her attention was focused on her niece, accusing, resentful. The girl's eyes were on the floor and there was a rigidity to the small body that amused me. I knew what she was thinking and it flared out soon. Bud bent his head to kiss the top of hers and said, "That does it, honey, now where's our room?"

She lifted her head high. "I'll show you. Sam, you come too. You'd better spend the night here." She twisted out of Bud's arm and marched out of the office.

Bud lifted a puzzled eyebrow and shoulders at me and we followed her. We were barely in the hall and I was putting my gun away when she whirled on us in fury.

"You miserable tricksters," she hissed. "Making me think I could trust you and all the time you were playing Mike Brown's game. Oh, I could just . . ."

Bud didn't give her time to say what she could just. Before she could jump out of reach he had grabbed her and covered her mouth with his, holding her until she quit fighting and sagged limply in his embrace. Then he took her face in both hands, his face still close to hers.

"Easy . . . easy, darling. Don't be fooled. I had to make Bill think that. If he didn't I'd be dry-gulched before daylight and you'd be a widow. If I'm going to help get the herd north and get your money we have to use Brocious and his crew, and I can't stay awake twenty-four hours a day to watch our backs. Believe me, Anne Marie. Believe me, please."

She shivered, a violent shudder, and her breath rushed out, her eyes begged him. "I don't know. I'm so mixed up. I guess . . . I hope you mean that."

His smile looped up to win her over. "Cross my heart. Give me time to prove it. Let's go to the room."

She looked from Bud to me and blushed. "I'll give you time if you give me time. This is all too fast." She turned and walked rapidly on down the hall and pushed open a door. "You two stay here," and without pausing started away.

Bud caught her hand and stopped her. "Uh-uh. You're not staying alone tonight. I won't touch you but we're all staying together. Your aunt has all the keys and tonight will tell whether she or Brocious will play along or try for murder."

The long strain of living with the people in this house since her parents' death was finally too much. She put her head against Bud's chest and wailed, a low, desperate sound, her knees beginning to fold. Bud caught her, lifted her, and carried his wife over the threshold of the room.

There was one big bed, a chest and a chair. I turned down the cover and Bud tucked the girl in, brushed her forehead with his lips, and she was asleep before he straightened. He looked at me, a brooding glare, then shrugged and spread his hands.

"Flip you for the first watch."

It was a mighty uncomfortable situation for me but I managed a warped smile. "I'll take it. You're going to need your sleep."

The next two days were hectic and I hardly saw him. There had been no attempt on either Anne Marie or Bud so I judged that Curly Bill had really bought the deal. I was back at the branding fire but Bud was busy with books and tallys.

News of the marriage spread and the Mexican community threw a fiesta. In the bunkhouse the crew gossiped in bafflement. The jokes were coarse, mostly about a shotgun wedding, but after the first day the bully Lemon threatened to take on the next man who made a crack.

"Knock it off, you guys. There ain't one of you wouldn't have tried for her if you hadn't been afraid of Mike Brown. Gilbert didn't scare."

Pete, the last man to have made a jibe, spat on the floor between his feet. "What I don't see is why Mike let him get away with it. Hell, he was boss man. How come a stranger can ride in here and not only grab off the kid but the ranch as well?"

Slim called from his table, "Maybe he ain't a stranger. She was down in Chihuahua; maybe they got together down there. What about it, Sam?"

I said, "It's none of my business or yours. Why don't you let it alone?" The way I still felt about Anne Marie I'd had my work cut out keeping my temper until now, and it told in my voice.

Slim was quick to try to cool me down. "Ah, Kid, don't get your dander up. A man's got to have something to talk about. We got nothing down here but dust and cactus. Your partner's all right, a hell of a fighter. Maybe that's why Mike didn't jump his frame."

"Maybe." I wasn't going to give them any information. Not that I had had any since the wedding night, and I was getting edgy at not having heard from Bud.

It wasn't until the next day, after the noon meal, that I had word. The same young Mexican Anne Marie had sent for us before caught me as I came out the door, smiling and saying the new Señor wanted me. We rode to the Mexican community and he pointed out a little adobe washed with bright pink lime. I went into a small room surprisingly clean, with whitewashed walls and a bright serape on the earth floor. Bud and Anne Marie sat at the hand-hewn table eating chili and beans with tortillas. It hurt to see her, fresh and glowing with a new deeper serenity in her eyes. She was obviously a married woman and feeling safe and loved.

Bud grinned, disgustingly smug, and introduced an old Mexican sitting cross-legged on the floor against the wall. "Pedro Navarro, Kid, the *Jefe* here. He speaks good English, don't you, Pedro?"

White teeth flashed in the lined Indian face. "The Señorita . . . Señora, teach me. *Buenos dias*, Señor Stewart."

Bud said, "There's only five or six hundred more cattle to brand and the boys can handle that. I want you to go with Pedro and meet the vaqueros who'll ride with us. There'll be twenty of them and two drivers, one for the carriage the ladies will ride in and one for their baggage wagon."

That was going to be some cattle drive. Ten thousand animals, many of them wild strays. Twenty or so American outlaws, most with prices on their heads. Twenty Mexican vaqueros with no experience herding cattle. Two women. All piling up a trail through rough country riddled with deserters from the various armies of the so-called Mexican Generals, and with Apache bands that the American army posts were supposed to keep on the reservations but who broke out and raided south whenever they took the notion. And with Curly Bill Brocious to watch and maneuver across the line. It would be no picnic.

Pedro Navarro got up with a little effort, bowed me out and followed, pausing in the hot sun to put on his wide sombrero. Barefoot, he led me down the dusty road where dark children played and dogs yapped, where Indian faces peeked at us out of unglazed windows. I stopped him as he began to turn in at a pale faded-blue house and spoke to him in Spanish, not trusting his understanding of English. I had to make it clear to him why the girl they were loyal to had married the American, that it was the only way she could keep the ranch from being stolen. I impressed on him that if anything happened to Gilbert, say he caught a stray bullet, the girl would lose the ranch and probably the Mexicans would lose their homes. It was, I said, up to him and his riders not to relax their vigilance for a minute. I told him I would keep as close to Gilbert as I could, but on a cattle drive there were a thousand ways a man could be killed.

He listened, watching me with flat, unreadable eyes, then changed his mind about going from house to house, yelled at the children and sent them scampering to gather fathers and brothers in the little plaza. It is hard to judge the age of these people, but the oldest of those who listened to the *Jefe*'s excited speech could not be more than twenty-five and some were just coming out of boyhood. They listened attentively but grinned and pushed at each other, and I knew they thought they were going on a lark—kids who had never been off the ranch in their lives and looked forward to seeing the world, just as Bud Gilbert and I had started out six years before. I put more faith in Bud's deal with Brocious than in this guard, but there was little security in that either.

Three days later we lined out. Three Americans ahead as lookout, then the women in their carriage, the wagon with their tent and baggage, and three chuck wagons, one for Brocious's crew, one for the vaqueros, and the third loaded with barrels of water.

Behind these, a quarter of a mile apart, were the two point riders. Their province was to keep the head of the herd moving in the right direction, keep it from swerving to one side or the other. Behind them the flankers were spaced along the great serpent of cattle. Last in the line rode the vaqueros, delegated to handle the horse herd (a good-sized remuda itself), with two spare horses for each man. That was the most miserable job, eating dust all day.

I did not like their being so far from Anne Marie and the first time I could catch him alone I suggested to Bud sending four of the older

Mexicans to ride beside the carriage, never to leave it alone.

I had to give points to Curly Bill for managing the unwieldy train. He was everywhere he was needed as the men turned the animals out of the huge holding pasture and pointed them northeast to cut the Chihuahua–El Paso trail. To a greenhorn it would look like chaos, but with the expertise of long practice the train was started on the seventy-five-mile trek to the border.

It would have been easier if the herd was split into sections, easier to handle three thousand head than ten. They could have been moved faster and it would not take so long to start them in the morning or bed them down at night. And in case of trouble, a stampede or attack, not so many would be involved. But Bill wanted to keep his crew together so he could throw out a screen of fighters and have men enough left to control frightened cattle.

We weren't going to set any mileage records. Ten or twelve miles a day is tops in moving a mass that size and most of the time five would be a good average. A cow is naturally slow, more interested in what grass tufts it can find and a drink from a running stream than in going anywhere. Bill had told Bud he hoped to be bedded just below the border within the week, which I thought was too optimistic.

But we did move. The herd was a ragged

quarter of a mile across and a mile long. Brocious patroled the west side and Bud worked back and forth along the east. I stayed fifty yards behind him, watching the flankers as he passed them, but there was no trouble the first two days.

By then the herd had shaken down and as usual a few of the animals had elected themselves leaders while the bulk were content to plod along behind them. One of these was a gaunt black steer with horns that wouldn't go head-on through a barn door. A suspicious beast, it viewed the world with alarm and would spook at the slightest sign of surprise. On the third day we got the surprise, and without warning.

We were weaving through a line of low, irregular hills that chopped the land into gullies and hogbacks. Those of us near the middle of the herd could not see either end of it. Pete was ahead of me when he stood up in his saddle, pointing at the mouth of a small canyon and yelling, waving his hat in the signal for trouble.

From where I was I couldn't see past the fringe of trees into the canyon, but when I spurred up to him there were riders coming down it. There were fifteen or more in sight and more appearing from around a bend.

"Get Mike," I said. "I'll take this side."

Pete wheeled his horse and picked a careful way across the moving herd while I watched the canyon. There was now double the number of riders I had seen first, half a mile away and coming fast. I could make out sombreros, so they were Mexican, not Apache, and from the bulky look of the bodies I guessed they wore bandoliers crossed over their chests. We didn't have much time to get ready for them. I kicked my horse toward the head of the herd. Bud had ridden up that way half an hour before and not come back.

The first flanker I passed I sent driving back along the herd to send the riders below us up to the canyon mouth and the rest I sent down to it.

"Bunch up. Keep them away from the cattle until Mike and Bud get there, but for God's sake don't shoot or the cattle will run."

I paused at the point rider, told him what was happening and left him to guide the animals, then I drove on to catch the carriage. Bud's horse was tied behind it and Bud was riding comfortably with the ladies. He heard my running horse and looked back, calling, "What's up?"

"Come on," I told him. "It looks like the whole rebel army."

CHAPTER TWELVE

Curly Bill was already at the canyon mouth when I got back there with Bud. He had about fifteen Americans with him, and half the vaqueros were racing along the side of the herd. The Mexicans were out of the canyon, fanned along the hill in a curving line.

There were nearly sixty, a ragtail outfit in ragged clothes and broken hats, on sorry horses. Bandits or deserters, whichever, their pickings had been lean of late, but their carbines were polished and their bandoliers full of ammunition.

Bill's crew was ranged behind him and when Bud got there the two of them walked their horses out from the rank and sat waiting for the Mexican's move. A squat, very dark man sporting a fierce handlebar mustache rode to meet them with two of his outfit. I kept back to watch our outlaws, figuring that if a fight developed somebody might decide to make points with Brocious by knocking Bud out of his saddle.

The Mexican trio stopped ten feet from Bill and Bud and the squat man called in a loud voice, in English not good but understandable.

"*Buenos dias*, Señors. May I present myself, General Huira, at your service."

On the horse next to me Lemon laughed and

said from the corner of his mouth, "And I'm the King of England."

Neither Brocious nor Bud spoke and the Mexican looked annoyed, shrugged, and announced, "I am Governor of this province and as such it is my duty to collect a tax from everyone using this road. For cattle the tax is one dollar a head."

He did not say what province he meant, and he certainly had not been governor of Chihuahua when Bud and I had been there so few days before. But these days any Mexican with a gun was prone to promote himself. And a dollar a head meant ten thousand for the herd.

Bill Brocious bowed in his saddle. "Excellency, there is some mistake. I hold a paper signed by the President of Mexico permitting me to drive cattle tax-free above the line."

I didn't know whether that was true or not, but neither did the General. He thought it over, then called up his two lieutenants and conferred with them in low tones. Our crew was restless, watching the long Mexican line, both sides holding their guns across their knees, ready. Behind us the cattle flowed on in a peaceful tide that would break into a thundering rampage if a volley exploded between the canyon sides, and I held my breath for the result of the conference. When it came it didn't sound good.

"Señor," the General called, "we cannot accept such a paper because we do not recognize the man who claims to be President of the Republic. My men will count your cattle and collect the legitimate tax."

Before he had finished Brocious flung up a hand and the American guns swung, every one trained on the General. Bill called, in Spanish better than the Mexican's English, "You are dead, Excellency, at the first move your men make."

The Mexicans hadn't been quick enough. Only a few had their guns on us and none of those was trained on either Brocious or Bud, they were aimed at their opposite numbers. The odds were overwhelmingly on their side but we had the drop on their leader. He craned his head around to both sides expectantly, then looked back to Brocious, sputtering.

"You wouldn't dare fire on a General."

Bill's laugh was heavy but without humor. "You willing to gamble your life on that? Try it and you'll be a sieve."

He waited while the General pondered the chance. The moment hung. There would be a massacre on both sides if Huira decided to take the risk. A massacre and a stampede that would send ten thousand cattle in panic up the trail, overrunning Anne Marie's carriage, leaving kindling and bloody pulp in their wake. And there was not a thing either Bud or I could do about it. It all depended on a Mexican bandit's guts or brains.

If he were going to challenge Brocious he should not have hesitated. I suspected that what went through his mind was a knowledge of what he would have done if the positions were reversed; ordered the murder without a second thought.

He waited too long. I saw the stiffness go out of his back. He lifted his shoulders and spread his hands, palms out in the most eloquent of Latin gestures, leaving the carbine across his knees.

"Yes. You would shoot me. Americans do not appreciate the nobility of a Mexican General. But we need money. Will you pay us something to let you go in peace?"

Bill Brocious guffawed. "You let *us* go in peace? You're lucky that I'm going to let your crowd ride out. You're staying with us. Tell your lieutenants to take your string back up that canyon. I don't care where they go as long as they stay away from the herd. The minute they come back within a mile of us I'll stake you bare-assed over an ant hill like the Yaquis do." He paused to let that sink in, then stepped his horse to Huira's side, took the carbine off the General's lap, the gun out of his holster and the knife from the back of his neck, and moved away.

"Give the order, General. Now."

Huira's play was finished. He gave the order and took out his frustration in cursing the lieutenants for being slow to obey. The lieutenants would have chosen to shoot it out with us even at the peril of their leader, then they flashed grins across at us, saying as plainly as words that there would be another time, wheeled their horses and galloped up the canyon with the ragged line behind them.

Bud Gilbert crossed to take the pair of bandoliers off the General's shoulders and feel over him for hidden weapons. He found another gun shoved in the belt under the blousy shirt and a second knife in a boot top, leaving Huira looking more shrunken with each loss, looking naked.

Curly Bill Brocious backed his horse to my side and grinned at me. "He ain't so tough now, Kid. Take him on back to the drag and hold onto him in case we need him."

I didn't like that, didn't like leaving Bud with only the vaqueros to look out for him, but neither did I want to refuse the foreman, make him suspicious or give him ideas he might not already have. I rode to him and Huira, passed him a message with my eyes and told him, "Brown says I'm to take the General to the back."

"*Vaya con Dios*," Bud said. "You worry too much."

Huira was looking wistfully after the last of his band just disappearing around the bend and I said, "If you're thinking you can make a break for it it's only fair to tell you I can shoot you before you get ten feet, and I will."

"Oh, I will not, Señor." He gave me a sudden crooked smile. "At least I will have a full belly for a change, I think. Everywhere we have gone there have been others before us. This country is picked clean."

We rode toward the rear, with the flankers dropping off at intervals, and turned around behind the remuda. For the next three days I ate dust and listened to the General spin tales of adventures, true or not, as a young lieutenant in the armies of the Emperor. He seemed unconcerned to be a prisoner and it was more entertaining to listen to him than to ride beside the bawling animals ahead of us.

During the days we rode side by side and at night we ate chili and tortillas with the vaqueros, who listened to him in silent awe. Then I tied his wrists and ankles with a rope looped through them to my wrist to rouse me if he tried to get up.

We made better time than I had expected. The weather was with us, with no heavy storms, and the graze was sparse but adequate. We saw only a few straggling riders at a distance and these gave us a wide berth. I didn't see Brocious or Bud until we were only fifteen miles from the line; then they rode back to us together, appearing thick as thieves, to my relief.

Brocious looked across me at the General and said, "Pull away, Mex. Head south. I've had a man backtracking and he says your army is about ten miles behind."

Huira's eyes lighted and he lifted his sombrero in a salute. "*Gracias*, Señor, I can find them before night."

"They may find you," Bill said casually. "I'm going to shoot you, but I want you far enough from the herd that a shot won't spook the critters."

The handlebar mustache quivered and the General's swarthy face turned a dirty grey. Brocious let him sweat, then his heavy laugh startled me almost as much as a shot would have.

"Scared you, didn't I? My man didn't see any sign of yours within thirty miles, so *vaya con Dios* and don't try to pick on any more Americans. They won't be as generous. Sam, you ride with him about five miles, then bring his horse back, put him afoot."

The Mexican groaned but did not try to argue with this foreman of the grisly humor. He nodded to me and turned his horse, sunk in his long, spiked spurs and drove south. Maybe he thought he could outrun me and keep his horse, but I was well mounted and stayed only a length behind him. His horse finally slowed, then dropped to a walk, and after six miles I came up beside him and told him to get down.

He stopped but didn't budge and I could see the wheels turning in his head, trying to guess whether I would actually shoot him if he refused. I took out my gun and cocked it.

He said hurriedly, "Señor, a canteen at least. I would die of thirst."

I nodded and he took the can off his saddle horn and shook it. It sounded almost empty.

"You can fill it at that stream we crossed this morning. Now get down and start walking."

He got down and stood back, for the first time showing ugliness, baring his teeth. "Adios, gringo. Until we meet again." He didn't warn me to watch myself; his face said it for him, and he was being a little careful with my gun on him.

I watched him walk a hundred yards, not looking back, then I tucked a lead rope through the reins of his animal and rode after the herd.

The cattle had made about a mile while I had ridden more than ten, and the dust still hung in the air for half a mile behind the remuda. I unsaddled Huira's horse and turned it in with the others, very glad to be shut of the General and free again to think about conning Brocious over the border. Pedro Navarro was there with the other vaqueros keeping the horse herd together and stopped beside me.

"I hope you killed that one. He is a bad man."

"Nope. Orders were to let him go."

Pedro grunted in disgust. "Boss should have sent me with him. I would have cut his fat throat. He has killed many of our people and the government put a price on his head, but no one dares go after it. Mike Brown makes bad mistake. Watch what I say. Huira will find his bandits and come again for these cattle."

"I don't think he'll have time, Pedro, we're too close to the line."

He said in an ominous tone, "He will make time. He moves like a spirit."

"I'll tell Mike."

I left him and rode along the herd asking the flankers where the foreman was and about halfway up the river of cattle was told he was riding point on the west side. That was behind the carriage and wagons so I didn't have a chance to see Anne Marie. I hadn't seen her since the day we took the General and I missed it a lot, even though I was trying to put her out of my thoughts. Bud was riding the east point and waved across to me as I reached Brocious's side, but he did not come over.

Curly Bill chuckled at me. "You lose the Mex?"

"Uh-huh. He told me so long until we met again. And the *Jefe* of the vaqueros tells me we made a mistake, that he's got a bad reputation for turning up where he isn't expected. A bad hombre, he says."

"I didn't exactly think he was a preacher. But we've only got one more day to drive. He hasn't got time to connect with his boys and give us trouble again. And speaking of time—is there any reason you can't go over to El Paso?"

"Why should there be?"

"Well, the sheriff might be looking for you or something."

I didn't exactly lie. Let him think what he wanted. "Not in Texas."

"Good. I want you to ride on ahead and send a wire to Billy Lee. Tell him the critters will be bedded down tomorrow night and to send along his crew."

"Okay, but why not go yourself, have a night on the town? Bud can run the show if you tell him where to take the herd."

He had used me to get rid of Huira, and now this. He could have sent any of his regular crew. I thought maybe he was buttering up Bud, making it obvious that he trusted us.

"Sure he could," Bill grumbled. "But they got a federal paper out on me up there and I don't want to spoil the favor Earp did me when he said he killed me. I go over there it would be my luck to run into somebody who knows me."

I made the question casual. "Seems like some of the crew must know who you are. Doesn't that bother you any?"

"Naw. They know I got enough friends up there that they wouldn't last long if they peeped. Them who know me are all right, some rode with me. Some rode with Ringo and for old man Clanton or the McLowerys." He shook his head slowly in regret. "Kid, them were the days."

Yes, I thought, those had been the palmy days for the outlaws. Not even the Hole-in-the-Wall gang could compare with the cruelty, the brutality of Curly Bill and his kind.

I said, "Okay, I'm on my way, soon as I say goodbye to my partner."

He raised his eyebrows. "You not coming back?"

"Maybe, maybe not. I've had about enough of cows for a while. Getting a little hungry for a good stiff poker game and some bright lights. Who knows? When I've had a fling I might have to come back."

He laughed aloud. "I doubt that. But I can't pay you off until the herd is paid for."

I waved that away. "You don't owe me for half a month even. Call it on the house—a wedding present. I can make it up on one hand tonight."

"So long then, Kid, don't take any wooden nickels."

"I'll try not to."

I turned the horse before he could offer a handshake and rode across to Bud Gilbert.

CHAPTER THIRTEEN

I briefed Bud on the disposition of General Huira, Navarro's warning, and Curly Bill picking me as his emissary.

"I just hope Billy Lee's crew shows up before the General's crowd. You and Brocious might not be so lucky a second time."

Bud shrugged off the danger. He never had been one to worry. "So Brocious is too cagey to go up himself. Now how do we get him across? Kidnap him?"

"With the whole crew around him?"

"We've got the vaqueros, and they're spoiling to get a crack at him. They don't like him a bit."

On the drive I had gotten to know the Mexicans and like them. This was my job and I didn't want them getting killed on my account. Those young, quiet-spoken, green kids wouldn't have a chance against Curly Bill's gun-hardened outlaws.

I said so to Bud. "I'll have to come up with another way. Take care of yourself and Anne Marie. Tell her goodbye for me."

He looked surprised. "Aren't you going to do it yourself?"

"Why?"

He looked at my face, then away. "All right. Be seeing you."

I didn't answer. I honestly did not know whether I'd ever see him again.

El Paso was not much as a town—a clutch of 'dobe saloons and gambling halls around the plaza, dominated by the two-story hotel, and mud huts ranged along dust streets that ran out like fingers from the plaza—a hot hole on the river bank under a hill that hadn't a piece of brush or a blade of grass on it. There was brush along the river, but spreading back on both banks there was nothing except bone-dry desert.

As in all the border communities, the Americans were outnumbered a dozen to one by the Mexicans. The cattle business west of Texas had not yet developed much and the principal occupation of the Americans was gambling.

I went to the telegraph office and sent the wire to Billy Lee Parks. I didn't use an address because everybody in Tucson knew where he lived. There was another American loafing there and I waited with him until the answer came, along with one for him. He told me he was with a crew waiting to take over the herd.

Then I hunted up the United States Deputy Marshal for western Texas. David Hood had made a big name for himself chasing characters in the Cherokee Outlet before he was sent down here. I'd met him twice when I'd been dealing at Luke Short's place and he remembered me.

"Hello there, Cactus." He sounded friendly.

"Come down to teach the boys to play poker?"

He was tipped back in the chair at his desk, his boots crossed on the scratched top and a crooked black Mexican cigar bobbing between his teeth. He did not get up or offer a hand so I didn't bother with amenities. There was a straight-backed chair against the wall and I hauled it over, reversed it, and straddled the seat, crossing my forearms on the back and dropping my chin to them. I watched him until he got curious enough to almost ask why I was there, then I said, "What would you think if I told you Wyatt Earp got a story wrong? That he did not kill Curly Bill Brocious, that Bill is alive and mean as ever and right now he's about ten miles south of the Rio Grande?"

He looked at me with a stone face for a long while, then the cigar jiggled again. "I'd think you'd got a touch of sun. Everybody knows he's buried at Iron Springs."

"Everybody except Bill and the Tucson Ring and some of an army of outlaws working for him, getting rich off a Mexican ranch."

Again he was silent, his mind poking at the possibility. Gradually his eyes narrowed. He took his feet off the desk, took the cigar out of his mouth, studied it thoughtfully, then with an expression of disgust tossed it at the cuspidor and hit it.

"Whereabouts is this ranch?"

"In Chihuahua, seventy-five or eighty miles south."

He stood up and made a slow circle of the room, coming back to face me. "Then what's he doing close to the border?"

"We brought a herd up for the Tucson Ring to sell to the contractors for the army posts and reservations."

"Rustled?"

"Part of them belong to the Flying L, the Livingstone ranch. Part to some neighbors and the rest are strays that he pays eight dollars a head for to anybody who gathers them. There's a lot of stuff wandering around loose. You never dreamed of the mess the revolutionaries have made of northern Mexico."

"I've seen it. What are you doing with Brocious?"

"Sit down. It will take a while."

He did and I went over the history again. "Bill told me somebody tried to blackmail him and dollars to doughnuts it was Doc Danby," I finished.

"Could have been. But it could still be your father who killed the Doc."

"He didn't. I know he didn't."

Hood was a good policeman but he wasn't showing as much interest as I needed him to. He just shrugged off my insisting on Rob Stewart's innocence and said, "How you going to prove it?"

"If I can get Bill north of the line and scare him, threaten to turn him over to you, I hope to make him tell me who did shoot Danby."

"Make a deal? Let him go? Why tell me about it?"

My insides were tight and I was pressing. I leaned over the desk and pounded a fist on it. "If I can't talk him into coming I want you to take a posse down and bring him."

He grunted at me. "You're crazy, Kid. I can't arrest anybody in Mexico."

I guess I was a little crazy. With Brocious so close and not being able to touch him I was grabbing at straws. I said, "A reward—is there still a reward out for him?"

"No." Hood was aggravatingly laconic. "As far as the government is concerned he's dead. There isn't even a warrant out for him. If he did turn up in the States a new one would have to be issued."

"You can do that?"

"If you can prove Bill Brocious is really alive."

I stood up. "Let's take a ride."

He looked up at me from the chair. That was the only movement he made. "How many did you say he had with him?"

"Twenty-five Americans, twenty—"

"No thanks."

My temper got away and I shouted at him. "What the hell kind of a marshal are you?"

He didn't ruffle. "A live one, Sam, and I mean

to keep it that way. As long as Brocious stays in Mexico I can't touch him. I couldn't even extradite him. There's no government down there to appeal to."

I was getting nowhere. It was like arguing with a steer. There would be no help from Marshal David Hood. I slammed out of the office and stormed down to the White Elk saloon. I needed a drink and a place to think. The day was late but I couldn't even think about food. It would lie like a cannon ball in my stomach.

The big room was crowded, the tables filled, but one emptied while I was on my second drink at the bar and I grabbed it, taking my glass and a bottle with me. I sat worrying over my problem like a dog with a rancid bone. If I couldn't get at Brocious one way maybe I had better try another tack. I began thinking about who Curly Bill might have approached to get rid of the blackmailer.

Who knew that Bill was alive? Certainly Billy Lee Parks, who was buying cattle from the outlaw. But Parks' henchman Harry Bedso apparently did not. Or did he? He hadn't exactly said Bill was dead when I went to Parks' house; all he had told me was that he had not been at Iron Springs with Brocious.

Yes, Whitey Bedso could have killed Danby, he was capable of shooting a man in the back. But he was not the only candidate. It could be Bert Thorne. Thorne could have come up to

Danby without the gambler thinking anything about it. After all, Danby was then a dealer in the Turquoise Palace.

I tried other names, but at the back of my head was the likelihood that Brocious had sent word to Parks and Billy Lee had sent someone I had never heard of. My mind began blurring, jumping from one thing to another, and suddenly I knew that I was drunk. I couldn't remember how much tequila I had had, but combined with my frustration it hit hard.

I paid the bartender and went outside, but it was no help. I got my horse and rode to the livery, turned it over to the barn man and climbed up in the hayloft to sleep. The next thing I knew it was morning. Mid-morning, to judge by the heat. But at least the long night had cleared my head.

Below me I heard voices, and I rolled over to look down the ladder. The barn man was talking with Marshal Hood and the officer was saddling a big black horse, tying on a canteen, so he wasn't setting out simply to patrol the town. A hunch struck me and I waited until he rode out of the runway and turned south. Then I moved quickly, climbed down, saddled and left the barn.

The street was full of traffic, people doing their errands before the afternoon's oppressive swelter settled over them and the siesta hour ran all of them inside until dusk. And the road to Mexico was crowded. This close to the border the small

Mexican farmers hauled their produce over to El Paso because the desperados did not bother the area much and because they preferred American dollars, having no faith in the peso. They were coming in with their donkey carts loaded, a long string of them, keeping close to each other for whatever comfort company would give them.

I did not want to get close to Hood. I had glimpses of his tall figure above the crowd, and sure enough, he crossed the bridge, walking his animal out of the road, clear of the carts, a picture of sedate composure.

Far beyond him the clear air above the horizon was yellow with dust. That would be the advancing herd, about eight miles away off to the west of the road but close to it. I circled out behind some low hills, shook up my horse and came down on the cattle just as the point riders were passing. Bill Brocious was not one of them and I asked the man nearest me which side of the drive he was on and he told me this side. Up ahead of the carriage and the lookouts I saw the black horse come over the brow of a rise and saw Hood dismount and stand quietly on the far side of the cattle.

I put my horse in a run down the flank because time was getting short and found Brocious clear at the drag, bawling at the vaqueros. He interrupted himself long enough to say, "You lose your stake already?"

"I couldn't stand being away from these lovable steers."

He didn't laugh. Something had put him in a bad humor. I found out a minute later. He turned back to the vaqueros. Apparently they had got careless and let the horse herd veer off up a shallow canyon and it had taken an hour to comb them out of the brush. When he was through with the Mexicans he ordered them away, then asked me, "You send the wire?"

"And got one back. Parks has a crew waiting three miles out of town and one of them picked up a wire that we're here."

"Good."

"What do you do with the money when you get it? You don't take it back south with only twenty-five men to keep you from being robbed, do you?"

He looked astonished. "What do you expect, I'd bury it in the ground?"

"There are banks in El Paso." I made a mental note to tell Bud to be sure Anne Marie's share went into an American bank.

"You got to be kidding," Brocious grunted. "I keep mine where I can get at it."

"Oh. Of course. And that reminds me. You remember Dave Hood, the Deputy U.S. Marshal in El Paso?"

"Yeah. What about him?"

"I just passed him, standing out at the edge of the road watching the cows go by."

"He's what? In Mexico?"

"That's what I said. Maybe he's wondering whose they are, or maybe he's heard a rumor and come to see if it's true you're alive."

I had all his attention now. He roared, "Where in hell would he hear that?"

"How do I know? Maybe he went out to see what Parks' crew was camped there for. Some of them could have been drunk and made a slip."

Brocious glowered at me like a bull at a red cape. "Show me where he's at."

I nodded toward the head of the herd and we rode back. The herd was not strung out along the trail any longer. It was being turned into a big bowl to be held there. It was short of the river three miles, but this had been the second dry day and if the animals got a smell of it there would be no controlling them. The riders were having a busy time of it; the carriage and wagons had been pulled out of line, a camp was being made and a noon fire built.

I could see Hood standing across from the wagons watching the riders hurrah the herd between him and the camp. I told Brocious to get down and walk, and dismounted myself. Screened by the slow passing animals, we reached the nearest supply wagon and Brocious climbed a wheel, put an eye out beyond the canvas-covered bow, then dropped back to the ground, saying viciously, "That's Hood all right. I wonder if he does know."

"I could tell him."

His head came around fast. "What's that mean?"

"That I will tell him unless you make a deal with me."

His big hand dropped for his gun. I beat him. Mine was out before he touched the butt of his.

"Don't, Bill. I can fire all six shots before you could lift yours."

He gave me a sickly grin. Brocious wasn't used to anyone handling a gun better than he did. But he didn't relax.

"You gone loco? You ain't in no position to talk any kind of deal."

"I think I am. I can hold you here until the herd is past and walk you across to Dave Hood. Between us we could ride you straight over the border."

His grin widened. "What do you think my crew would be doing while we took that little ride."

"Look around. The crew is so busy turning those animals that even if some of them got wise we'd still have a good chance of making it. But Bill—I don't want to give you to Hood."

His face wiped empty. "You don't? I figured you were after the reward. What is it you do want?"

I didn't tell him there wasn't any reward. "Justice."

He laughed at me as I'd expected. I didn't know how many men he had killed aside from Marshal White of Tombstone, but if Mexicans were included he must hold a world record. Justice had no meaning to him. He had no moral sense at all, nor any conscience. Now with the word off my chest I had to find another way to appeal to him. It couldn't be money. He was taking more out of the cattle than anyone could want. But perhaps a rumor I had heard would turn the trick. He was said to have a special hatred of the warden of Yuma prison.

I said, "Justice for me. For you, what would you give to get a prisoner out of Yuma scot free?"

His eyes brightened and he licked his lips, then his mouth turned ugly and he grunted. "With double my full crew I wouldn't be fool enough to go up against that box. Do you know they've got a Gatling gun mounted on a platform that can cover the whole place? They could shoot up the Fourth Cavalry in an attack."

"I've seen it," I told him. "My father's in there because he confessed to killing Doc Danby. He didn't do it and you know who did. And why."

His face changed from astonishment at the word *confessed,* to a threatening glower. We watched each other through a heavy silence, then I broke the tableau by deliberately returning my gun to the holster. His eyes dropped to my hand, then came up again. He knew exactly what I was telling him, saying it louder than words would. I was saying that I was not going to take him over to Hood.

It was then that the big black horse stepped carefully through the river of cattle, stopped twenty feet from us, and Marshal Dave Hood spoke from the saddle.

"Morning, Bill."

I flipped the gun out again and held it on Brocious. I didn't want him shooting Hood and maybe we would take that ride after all, but it didn't work that way. The marshal simply sat there looking at the outlaw without expression. He seemed to be oblivious of me, but I knew he was aware of my gun. The next minutes were an hour for me. Then Hood turned the black, turned his back, and walked the animal away through the cattle again and turned north up the road.

CHAPTER FOURTEEN

It took all afternoon to get the herd spread out across the bowl. It was about two miles wide, nearly round, and by using all of it there would be enough feed and barely enough water in a little creek to keep the animals alive until they could be driven across. They crowded in to drink, trampling the stream to mud and it took the full crew, Americans and vaqueros, to keep them moving off after they had had a little water.

The camp had been set up at the northern end, close to the road, the tent for the women a hundred feet beyond the fire, by the time the crew began straggling in for supper in shifts, while the rest patrolled the herd.

Bud and I got there about the same time and we took plates to the tent. It was the first time I'd seen him to speak to since I'd got back from El Paso and I told him I had news. He had been eating with his wife and Carmen at the tent during the drive, but when we filled our own plates with beans and meat he walked off with me to a place apart, sat down on the ground and said, "Shoot."

I told him how I had contacted the marshal and how Hood had come down, faced Brocious and ridden home.

"You took a big chance, Kid. Supposing Hood

had spoken to you. It would have been a tip-off to Brocious that it was you who had let it out that he's alive."

"I had to risk it and Hood has a reputation for being smart. I couldn't see any other hope of getting Brocious into the States, unless we threw a sack over his head and kidnapped him."

Bud said between bites, "We might have done that."

"We still may, but I'm trying something else. I had him under the gun twice today and purposely let him off the hook. I've been studying him, thinking back. He's showed a stubborn loyalty all along. Remember how he stayed with his crowd even after that yellow-belly Ike Clanton double-crossed him? And he never double-crossed one of his own men, even when Ike tried to sell out to the Earps."

"I don't know what you're getting at."

"I'm gambling that Bill doesn't like to be under obligation to anyone. He is to me now. I warned him Hood was down here and I made sure he knew I wasn't going to turn him over when I had the chance—or when he thought I had the chance."

"I'd say it's a bad gamble. He's more apt to resent you for putting him in that spot."

"I'll have to wait and see."

"Yeah. Well, you'd better come sleep close to me tonight."

Bud rose and took his empty plate back to the chuck wagon and went on to the tent. He went in for a few minutes, then came out with his blanket and rolled up in front of the entrance. We were both tired. I had had all the riding I wanted for one day and I was glad I hadn't drawn night duty.

I was about to take Bud up on his invitation when I saw Curly Bill, near the fire, get up and go to the tent, step across Bud and put his head inside, then back out and go to the rope corral that had been strung for the night riders' horses. He saddled one and rode off toward the herd. I groaned, but it was too good an opportunity to miss. I saddled and followed him.

The animals were still thirsty and restless, half of them still on their feet in spite of the reassuring crooning of the circling riders. Bill was riding aimlessly, more as though he didn't know what to do with himself than as if he thought he was needed here. I was gaining on him slowly, not as if I intended it, singing in the soft monotone, pretending I had not a thing on my mind but the welfare of the cattle.

He finally heard me and turned, stopped, and sat hunched in saddle, in the early dark looking more like a hairy bear than a man. The light from a rising moon was fairly bright but it did not show my face under the hat brim, but he recognized my voice.

"Sam?"

I said, "Yeah."

"What are you doing out here? You're not due until morning."

I came up and stopped beside him. "Couldn't sleep. I've got the willies."

"You too? What about?"

"I keep seeing my father in that hell hole. It isn't fit for rats, let alone a man."

"So I hear. What the hell made him confess?"

"The woman he wanted was married to Danby. Doc had driven her to the point where she said she could kill him, and Dad thought she had. He did it to save her."

"Women."

In Brocious's mouth it was a curse and it surely wasn't love that kept him tied to Carmen Brown. We rode on, cutting slowly through the standing cattle, trying to quiet them, and found ourselves back at the fire. We got down and poured hot coffee from the huge pot set against the coals and stood drinking. There was no one else awake in the camp. Those who weren't riding were dark shapes in blankets scattered off away from where they would be disturbed by men stopping off at the fire.

Brocious rumbled in his throat and said, "So you did come to Mexico looking for me. I thought so in the first place."

"Not you. I want the man who killed Danby. You can tell me who."

"Sure. I paid him five thousand for the job, to get that picture I told you about. And the fool didn't find it."

I said softly, "Because Danby gave it to his wife. I got it from her."

I watched him closely but he didn't want to draw on me again. He was silent, thinking, sucking greedily at the hot coffee. He turned his back, walking over to put the cup back on the tailgate of the cook wagon and said from there, "It ain't important anymore, now Hood's seen me. I just still got to stay down here. But I'll make a deal with you if you do something for me. Tell that partner of yours to get on his horse and light a shuck."

I should have expected that but I had overlooked it. It was a couple of minutes before I could absorb it and answer.

"If I do and he does, what then?"

"I'll tell you who got Doc Danby."

I gave him a short laugh. "What good will that do me? How do I prove it?"

He came back, the moon catching his big teeth through a wolf grin. "I've got the letter he wrote to tell me Danby was dead and he couldn't find the photo, and wanting the second half of the five thousand I'd promised him. Is that enough for you?"

"I doubt it." I was disappointed. "Anybody I took it to could say it was a forgery."

"Uh-uh. He signed it with his name and a thumb print with a V scar on it so I'd know it was him. You take his body to the law and they'd have to believe it."

The hair on the back of my neck stood up, prickling. I said, "His body? Dead?"

"Dead. Let's find out just how bad you want your pappy out of that cell. I want him paid off for botching the job and I don't have anybody up there who would do it."

That sounded to me as if it were someone under the protection of the Tucson Ring and I gave him a flat laugh.

"And the next thing, I'd land in the same cell with my dad. Thanks for nothing."

"No you wouldn't. Who do you think makes the law in Arizona? Billy Lee Parks. He owns the Governor. You show him that letter and I promise you won't even stand trial. Your father will come out of Yuma with a full pardon."

I knew Parks could do all of that, but again I laughed at Brocious. "Sure . . . Sure. You promise. But Billy Lee won't send someone to do the chore you're asking me to do. I think he wouldn't like me for doing it, so why would he do anything for me? He'd have me hung for murder before I could wink."

Brocious stuck out his lower lip and stared at me for a long moment, then he swore. "You're pretty damn sharp, aren't you, Stewart. Well, there's another way. The Ring can't control the federal people. Take the letter to somebody like Dave Hood. Say the guy pulled a gun on you when you tried to arrest him and you killed him in self-defense. They won't do a thing to you and they'll get your pappy out in a hurry. How about that?"

My heart hammered so loud I thought Brocious must hear it. The result he talked about was just what I wanted, but the price was far too high. I wouldn't mind facing the man who had shot Danby in the back, or killing him. It was the first part of the condition I was thinking of. The girl. If Bud Gilbert did ride away it would leave her back in the hands of her aunt and Brocious.

I stood there with my father's freedom and a clear name practically in my pocket. I tried to tell myself that he was more important than Anne Marie, but I couldn't make it work. I squirmed like a worm on a fishhook while he watched me with the satisfaction of a gambler who's just drawn his fourth ace. I drew a breath that came out in a ragged shudder and said, "There's one hitch. I don't own Bud Gilbert. I'd be lying if I claimed I could make him do what he doesn't want to do, and he's in love with his wife. He won't leave her no matter what I say."

Curly Bill walked to his horse, swung up and

looked down on me. "Your problem. You want that letter, get Gilbert away. You don't even get a look at the letter until he's gone."

He kneed the horse and rode back to the herd, which was still not fully bedded. There was a core that continued jostling for position at the creek, bawling when they could not get to the water. I took my animal back to the rope corral, unsaddled, then went to the tent and touched Bud's shoulder.

His eyes opened at once. I beckoned him away from the tent and he rolled out and followed me to the fire. He didn't ask questions, waiting until I poured coffee for him and told him, "I've just been made an interesting proposition by Curly Bill. He offered me the name of Danby's killer and a letter reporting the murder, one that can be confirmed."

He threw a light punch at my shoulder. "Great. What's he want in trade?"

"Not much." I threw the words away lightly. "Only that I shoot the killer—and one other little thing. That I get you to ride out alone and not come back."

He was sipping at the coffee. He took it away from his lips and held the cup, unconscious of it, letting it tip and spill without noticing it.

"Not much did you say? I don't care who you kill, but did you agree to work on me? Kid, I am not going to leave Anne Marie. Not even to help your father. Don't ask me to or you and I have had it."

"You know I wouldn't. That's why I waked you, to warn you. I told him you were stubborn and loved your wife. I didn't like the way he took it. I think you'd better get her up and slip her out, take her to El Paso. If Carmen wakes up I'll help and we'll take her too."

He didn't hesitate a second. "She wouldn't go, Kid. We both want to be around when that cattle money is paid over."

In the moonlight I could see the square set of his jaw. No matter that he could now more than ever expect a bushwhacking, Bud Gilbert would not run. He never had learned how. I kept trying, arguing that there was no great rush for me to leave, that I could stay and keep track of the money, telling him that when it was paid to Brocious I could watch my chance to waylay him, knock him out, get the money and the letter and meet him in El Paso.

He was listening but not convinced, and I was getting hot under the collar that he was so bullheaded, when shots, a lot of them, and a loud whooping of many voices broke over the camp.

Around us the riders scrambled out of blankets, kicked into their boots, snatched up their guns and ran for the horses. In the herd the animals on their feet threw up their heads, looking for the direction from which the frightening noises came, and those lying down thrashed up, an electric current of terror spreading through them. They began milling in a quickening swirl, suspicious, not yet knowing which way to run.

It sounded to me as if the attack was south of the camp, about midway of the bowl. Bud and I were already racing, he for the tent, which would be in the path of a stampede northward, I toward the horses.

Nothing is more terrible than a cattle stampede. Floods are bad, a wall of water churning down an arroyo will flush everything before it, but there is a chance if it catches you that you will be cast up and possibly land on a ledge safely. But forty thousand hoofs crowding together in a pounding run will trample everything under. Even a rider on horseback isn't safe. The sharp horn of a frenzied steer can debowel a horse with a single hook, and there is no way to out-ride the cattle. The wide horns interlock in a web that cannot be ridden through.

I fought through the men who were hurriedly throwing saddles on the horses, without apology grabbing the reins of two ready to mount, yelling that they were for the women. The man from whom I took the second animal cursed me and tried to beat me off but I hit him hard with the back of my arm and he stumbled out of my way.

I swung up and, towing the other horse, drove for the flimsy tent. Bud had the two women outside, in their nightgowns. He lifted Carmen in his arms and heaved her up in front of me, flung into the other saddle, reached for Anne Marie and hauled her into his lap, shouting at me. "Ride for the river."

I did not need to be urged. Already the cattle were on their way, the milling over, the leaders running toward us. In minutes the rest would follow, trying to escape the shots and yells that continued behind them.

As we drove out I looked back to see how much headstart we had and was in time to see the vanguard hit the water wagon, the chuck and supply wagons, and then the tent and carriage beside it. They went over the camp in a wave of destruction. Everything vanished under the charge, and the rising drumming of hooves and clacking of horns roared like a frightful tempest.

We did not follow the road but headed for the bend that dipped down closest to us. It was still nearly three miles and the horses were tiring under the double loads by the time we reached the bank. We slid them down and kicked them through the brush fringe and into the river. It was low, the water not belly high, and we splashed to the other side and up the far bank. We stopped to rest there, watching the cows beginning to pile up as they hit the water, pausing in their flight to drink. Some were overrun, trampled to death; some were pushed across by those behind. But most spread out both ways, not plunging on but dropping their thirsty heads.

Bud sounded more than disgusted. "That's that. If it weren't for the river they'd have run plumb to Montana."

CHAPTER FIFTEEN

We took the women to the El Cortez, where the manager found Mexican skirts and blouses for them and gave them a room. Then Bud and I rode back to the river. The noise of the stampede had waked the whole town and a lot of the people were running south to gawk at the show. There had never been a herd of this magnitude gone mad so close to them before.

From the north bank we looked across at dead animals trampled at the water's edge by the thundering wave behind. The wide, shallow stream was still filled with live cattle spreading east and west, but nothing in sight would total ten thousand head or anywhere near it. There were riders gathering up small bunches and hazing them back toward the bowl, but in the short time that had passed they could not have collected a major number.

Bud swore aloud. "Where the hell are they all?"

In the grey pre-dawn light I could just make out the silhouette of the low hills across the river. "Maybe in the dark they split and some went up the draws. We'll have a lovely time combing them out of that mesquite."

"Yeah. And we can use that crew camped north of town. Kid, you ride up and bring them while I get the boys here organized. I can't see Brocious around, can you?"

The big foreman was not in the river nor in sight on the other bank. I left Bud to take over and turned my horse north, but I hadn't gotten through the little town when I heard running hooves and saw a group of twenty or so Americans come down the trail in a rush. I stopped and waited until they reached me, with Whitey Bedso riding in the lead.

He spotted me, held up a hand to halt the crew, and rode to my side, sounding surprised.

"The Cactus Kid!"

"Hello, Whitey. Have you heard what's happened?"

"Yeah. One of my boys spent the night in the cantina and rode out to tell us. What are you doing here?"

"Riding herd."

"Curly B . . . Mike Brown. Where's he at?"

"God knows. I haven't seen him lately." I took no notice of the name he had started to use, but now I knew for sure he had been in on the secret. I could have saved us all a lot of effort if I'd wormed it out of him in the beginning.

"But what are you doing in El Paso? Last time I saw you was at Billy Lee's when he gave you the Turquoise faro bank. What happened to that?"

"Bert Thorne." I made my voice savage. "The bastard sent a couple of men to hold us up and grab our bankroll. I couldn't run the game without money."

We measured each other, Bedso showing suspicion before he said, "Why didn't you come back and tell Billy Lee?"

"I kill my own rats, but without dough there was nothing we could do so we headed into Mexico to look for a stake, ran into Brown and came up the trail with the herd."

"We? You and who else?"

"Bud Gilbert, my partner—or he was my partner before he married the girl who owns the ranch."

Bedso's voice rose on an incredulous note. "Anne Marie Livingstone? Well I'll be damned."

In the growing light a whole chain of thoughts chased themselves across the back of Whitey's eyes. I wondered how much he knew about the Livingstone operation, if the Tucson Ring wasn't more deeply involved than merely buying cattle from Curly Bill.

I said, "Let's get on across the river and start work. There's plenty to do to put this herd back together."

He signaled his crew and we rode, but there was a change in Harry Bedso. He had always been friendly to me and now there was a reserve, a chilliness I didn't understand.

There was also a change in Bud Gilbert when we came up with him. He was a different man than I had grown up with, his devil-may-care attitude gone and replaced by a hard, driving strength as befitted the manager of the Flying L. He greeted Bedso with a short nod and said first thing, "Did you bring the money?"

Bedso's eyes went to the dead animals being snaked out of the river and he snorted. "It's in the El Paso bank, but from the look of things here we won't need so much."

Bud's jaw thrust out in quick anger. "We lost a few but most of them are still alive."

"All right, all right." Bedso backed away a step. "There wasn't any storm last night, so what spooked them?"

I cut in. "A Mexican bandit general tried to hit us down the way. We ran off his gang and put him afoot. I think they got together again and came back."

Bedso lifted his shoulders. "And they probably ran off a jag, maybe a lot."

"If they did we'll get them back." Bud sounded serenely confident and I was caught again by the sense of leadership that had come over him overnight.

And I could see that in spite of himself Harry Bedso was impressed. He had run Billy Lee Parks' errands for a long time and very little impressed him.

"Let's get started," he said. "You can work my crew while I go find Mike Brown."

"I'll go with you," I told him. I wanted to be there when those two talked together.

We turned toward the bowl where the camp had been. All along the way we saw bunches of cattle being held or not yet picked up, standing exhausted by their hard run, nibbling at what grass tufts had survived the hooves. The riders were working haphazardly, with no one giving orders, and I stopped a pair near the road and asked where Mike Brown was. Neither of them knew. I told them, "Take your gathers back to the bowl and stay there with them. Tell the other boys as they come in to keep looking, check the draws and gulleys for anything that turned off."

One of the riders spat on the ground. "We ain't et and we can use some coffee, but there's nothing left of the camp."

Harry Bedso said, "I brought a chuck wagon; it ought to be on this side of the river by now."

The riders looked to me, as the boss's partner, for permission, and I said, "Go on up, then. Get some grub and tell Bud Gilbert how things are down here."

One gave me a disgruntled glance. "How are they?"

I looked at him until his eyes fell, then they both headed back to the river. They had about two hundred head, just standing still. I told Bedso we would move them on to the bowl while we looked for the foreman, and we got them started, riding together behind them.

Bedso asked, "How many head did you have when you started?"

"About ten thousand. Ordinarily I wouldn't take Curly Bill's word but Bud read the tallys." I was getting tired of playing the name game.

Whitey's head snapped around and he stared at me; then he said, almost without sound, "So you know."

I pretended innocence. "What's so strange about that? I used to see him around Contention."

"And the day you came to see Billy Lee you asked me if I'd been with Curly at Iron Springs . . . Does Bill know you know him?"

"Sure."

He said nothing more, but while we pushed the cows along I caught him casting sidelong glances at me and knew he would bring it up with Brocious when we found him. I wondered what Bill would tell him.

I never found out. Curly Bill was dead. We discovered his body on the far side of the bedground midway of the bowl. He lay with one leg caught under his dead horse, with two bullet holes in his chest and another in his forehead, surrounded by powder burn.

But there were two other dead men with him, one lying across his body—Mexicans with bandoliers crossed over their shoulders.

I tried to picture what had happened. Huira's sixty bandits had come in whooping and firing and Brocious, with the brainless courage for which he had been noted, must have tackled them alone, had his horse shot out from under him, taken two slugs in the chest, and still had life enough left as the shot was fired into his head at point-blank range to fire his own gun into the man.

I swung down and tossed my reins to Bedso. The horses were skittish at the blood smell, which was getting strong in the rising heat, and he backed away. I kneeled beside the big body and went through the pockets. Curly had said I wouldn't see the incriminating letter until Bud Gilbert was gone, so I thought he must have it on him, unless he had left it in his bedroll. In that case all my chances were blown to hell. The paper would be shredded and buried in the churned dirt, and Bill could never tell me the name of the man I wanted. My hands shook as I fumbled with his clothes. There was nothing in the pockets except a few cigars in one and a handful of money in his trousers. In desperation I yanked open his shirt, but there was no thong around his neck with a pouch on it. I almost gave up, sick at my stomach. Then I caught a glimpse of leather against his bare belly. A money belt. My fingers were clumsy getting his pants open enough to unfasten the buckle and drag the belt out from under the heavy body, clumsy probing through the belt pockets. There was nothing but bills in them until I found one sewed closed where the belt would have touched his spine. And that was where I found the letter when I ripped the thread away.

That was all I took from the dead man. Kneeling with my back to Harry Bedso, I read the round, schoolboy script.

> Friend Bill, I caught up to Doc Danby like you said. I caught him in Tucson, all alone, so drunk he'd fallen down. I shot him twice, once in the back of his neck and once in his head. He never made a sound. Then I searched him. The picture of you wasn't on him. I went to the hotel where he was staying and went through his baggage. No soap. So I went back to Tombstone and searched his room at the boardinghouse and the locker he used at the Palace. No picture. I don't know where he kept it but I don't think you've got a thing to worry about. Doc wasn't the kind to share a secret with anybody. So if you'll send me the twenty-five hundred bucks you still owe me I'll be much obliged.
>
> Your buddy, Bert Thorne

I was so intent on the words that Harry Bedso's voice shocked me. His tone was acid, mocking.

"How much dough did you find on him, Cactus?"

I left the belt lying across Bill's fat, hairy belly and stood up. "I didn't count it, Whitey."

"Hand it up here."

If Bedso wanted to rob the corpse that was up to him. I stooped for the belt and tossed it to him, and in my turning he saw the paper in my hand.

"What's that? What did you take off him?"

I almost told him to mind his own business but a look at his eyes changed my mind. Bud Gilbert needed this man and his crew if he was to recover Anne Marie's cattle and get them sold. I stepped to his horse and passed the letter up. He read it, showing surprise and puzzlement.

"I'll be damned. Why would Curly want Danby dead?"

I told him about the photograph that indicated Bill Brocious had been alive long after the Iron Springs fight, and that Danby had tried to blackmail Brocious with it—told him I had found it, but not how.

His thin-lipped mouth looped up on one side. "And you was going to try the same thing when he got the cattle money?"

I reached for the letter and did not answer until it was safely in my pocket. "No, Whitey. My father is doing time in Yuma prison. He confessed to shooting Danby because he thought the woman he loved had done it. This will get him out."

Bedso poked his hat back from his forehead and his eyes turned reflective. "I see. Now things are beginning to make some sense. That's why you asked me if I was with Bill the day Wyatt Earp thought he killed him. And you wanted the Tombstone faro bank to snoop around, smoke Curly out. Billy Lee and me never really thought you was out to do Parks any favors, but telling him about the skimming was a good tip. When you disappeared Billy Lee sent word to Thorne and he ain't doing that anymore. But I can't see how that letter can do you any good. Thorne will just claim it's a forgery."

"I can prove it's genuine," I said, but I did not tell him how.

"How did you know Curly Bill had it, anyway? It ain't like him to be loose-mouthed."

"He talked in his sleep."

I wanted to get off the subject. I didn't like so many questions from Parks' henchman and this was a good time to stop them. Bud Gilbert and some of Bedso's riders were coming up. Bedso tossed me my reins and took his horse off to one side, where he sat concentrating on Bud as if he were measuring him.

Gilbert pulled in beside me and for a moment looked silently down on the dead outlaw, then raised his eyes to me, questioning. I gave him a bare nod. He got down, hitched his belt and walked to the body, saying, "So this is the real end of Curly Bill. Give me a hand with him, Sam." He raised his voice to the riders. "Some of you put a rope on that horse and drag it off him. I'll send a man down with a shovel if we can find one in the wreckage."

I bent with him to haul the body out from under the animal as the rope lifted the stiffening horse enough to free the leg, but Bud saw from my face that I didn't care whether Brocious was buried or not, and said in a low tone, "It don't matter to me, but I've got to live with my wife's aunt, and the old harridan is tough enough to get along with. I don't want her holding it over me that I left her husband's body for buzzard meat."

That was the first thing that made me feel at all good about the marriage and I couldn't resist rubbing in a little salt.

"Sounds like all is not bliss in the household. You'll have to take the bitter with the sweet, buddy boy. Maybe I was lucky after all."

"Sour grapes. Anne Marie and I get along fine."

I didn't want to hear anything about that and turned away. I wanted to show him Thorne's letter, but not in front of Bedso's crew, who all worked for the Ring. Some of them might be friends of the Tombstone gambler.

I walked to where Harry was talking to one of them and got there in time to hear him say, "Ride back to El Paso. Billy Lee is due in on the afternoon train. Tell him I'll meet him at the

El Cortez as soon as I know what the score is."

When the man had gone Harry showed me a doleful face, shaking his head. "I'm damn glad Billy's coming. With Brocious dead I don't know how the deal shapes up. I don't know who we're dealing with."

"Gilbert, of course. His wife owns the ranch." I didn't like the sound of what he had said, nor of what he said next.

"I got nothing but your word they're married. Maybe the pair of you are figuring on pulling a whizzer on Parks. There's a lot of money involved."

Harry Bedso and I had always gotten along and this sudden hostility had a meaning behind it. I thought I knew what it was and wandered off, back to Bud, who had changed his mind about a shovel and had the men piling rocks over Curly Bill. I winked at him and went on, out of earshot of the others. He followed me. We stood with our backs to the burial, looking across the bowl to where several teams of riders were pushing little jags of cattle in against the stream, leaving them there and going back for more. With the heat and roiling dust, I knew this extra work wasn't making Huira's Mexicans any more popular with either the Americans or the vaqueros, wherever they were. From where we were I couldn't locate one of them.

Bud said, "You find the letter?"

"In a minute. There's something else up. Billy Lee Parks is coming in on the afternoon train and I think Whitey Bedso is planning a switch. I've got a hunch that with Brocious out of it they'll think they can buy Curly's crew to throw in with Bedso's and try to grab the herd without paying anything for it."

Bud's jaw set in that stubborn line that meant he would fight the whole crowd single-handed if it came down to that, but before he could make any such stupid threat there was a volley of popping sounds out to the west of us.

Gunfire, a long way off.

Between the hills that made a low barrier on the west of the bowl there was an opening, a fairly steep, wide canyon, where last night Brocious had posted two men to keep the cattle from drifting up it. The sounds seemed to come down on the breeze from there.

Bud and I ran for our horses and Bedso raised a yell to call those of his men who were in the bowl, and in a ragged line we started for the canyon.

CHAPTER SIXTEEN

We were well up the grade, inside the mouth, barely able to hear the continuing shooting. Then it was drowned by a new sound, growing and terrible, the rolling, steady thunder of running cattle.

A moment later they came around the bend above us, the second stampede within twelve hours, the leaders wild-eyed, heads down, bearing down on us, great numbers of them in a surging flood. There were many horses among them from our remuda and I had a sick wondering about the fate of the young vaqueros.

About half of Bedso's crew and half of Curly Bill's had been working in the bowl. Those who had been closest to us were strung out in the canyon, but there were others still on the flat, driving through the cows down there. When these heard the pounding hooves they would also run and some of the men would be caught. Their only chance would be to turn, go with the stampede as it closed around them and hope their horses could keep their footing.

We in the canyon had to climb, and fast. Bud swept his arm toward the slope nearest us and we kicked the horses up it at an angle, the riders behind us following, getting out of the path of the cattle with seconds to spare. Up out of danger we paused and watched the flood go by. It looked like half the entire herd.

Bud signaled again and we moved on up along the side of the curving hill. Gradually it steepened and we had the choice of dropping back into the seething mass of cows or turning sharply up to the ridge. Once on the ridge, we found that it twisted away from the canyon, the slope developing into an almost perpendicular wall broken by narrow shelves, and still cattle swept by below us. The canyon bottom narrowed, forcing the animals into a thin line that gradually dwindled out.

The last echo of the drumming of hoofs faded and we could hear over it again the gunfire, louder, closer, higher than we were. We waited until all the riders who had made it up the slope were with us, twenty of us, then rode on up the ridge, unable to get down without going back a mile.

The spine of the hill kept turning one way and then the other in a snake-like course. The canyon bottom opened into a wide hill-valley, where I judged the cattle had been before they started running. There was no one down there now but the shooting was much closer, not a steady fire but an occasional shot, as if the opposing forces were hidden from each other most of the time.

We reached a place where the ridge veered sharply along the top of a secondary gulley dropping into the main canyon, and there the firing was loud, directly below us, and puffs of smoke picked out the locations of those shooting. One group was boxed at the head of the draw and another had the lower entrance blocked. Bud and I sat together watching and Harry Bedso pulled in beside us.

Bud said, "What do you make of it, Kid?"

I saw a sombrero move behind a rock where the upper group was pinned down, and someone in the lower group shook a serape into sight and drew fire.

"Two bunches of Mexicans at each other's throats."

Bedso said, "Yeah, but who are they?"

I said, "Could be a revolutionary argument but I think it's Anne Marie's vaqueros and General Huira's gang."

"Which is which?"

"Let's go down and ask them."

"And get a bullet in your gizzard."

I told him, "There are plenty of rocks for cover to get me in contact with the people holding the mouth of the sack. I think they're the vaqueros. I don't think Huira would bother nailing down a handful of Mexican kids. More likely he'd be after those cattle."

Bedso shrugged, saying, "What's the difference? They're all only Mex. Let them fight it out and let's get back to work with the herd."

I met Bud's eyes and knew he would like to run Bedso over the edge. He had taken quite a shine to the Mexican boys.

"Go to it, Kid. See if you can make it down on the lower side of them so if you're wrong we can lay down enough fire to keep them where they are while you work on out of the canyon. Give us a signal if you're right and we'll ride on up to flank Huira. We get him bracketed between us and the vaqueros, we can take him."

I got off the horse and walked to the rim, studying how the ground fell away. It did not look too bad here—bare of brush, but I thought I was out of range of the upper group. I went over the edge with my rifle in my right hand, using my left to hold onto rocks while I felt for firm footing in the descent. About thirty feet down the grade was steeper than it had looked from above, and it was a hundred feet to the ledge below. Then two unpleasant things happened. A rock I was trusting my weight to moved and was about to pull loose with my next step. And a bullet whined off the wall just below me.

I hung there like a spider at the end of a flying web. Other shots splintered rock chips too close for comfort. I had the choice of waiting until one hit me or dropping clear, with nothing to slow me down until I landed on the ledge, probably breaking bones. As a gambler I chose to drop.

I don't appreciate the sensation of falling. It probably goes back to an ancestor who fell out of a tree. I was lucky in landing in a patch of sand surrounded by boulders, but I hit so hard that I bounced, went over backward, and banged my head against stone. It all but jarred my teeth loose, but it did not knock me out and I had held onto the rifle.

Shots winged off the boulders and I slid down and sat on the sand waiting for my head to quit ringing and the lights to stop exploding behind my eyes. I became conscious of a voice calling, but it was a while before I comprehended that it was below me.

"Señor . . . Señor . . . Señor Stewart . . ."

I could not answer at once. My breath was knocked out. Then I managed to croak, "Who is it?"

"Pedro Navarro. Are you hurt bad?"

"I'm all right. Give me a minute. When I tell you, start shooting so I can come on down."

Gradually my senses steadied and I called to him, and when he started firing I looked around the boulder, discovered him in a rock cluster on the floor of the draw with only a twenty-foot slide through loose rubble between us. I went down it on my backside, scorching my pants and skin. He ducked down at my side and looked at me in wonder.

"The Señor has a hundred lives and has just used at least thirty of them. Maravilla."

"Nothing to it, *Jefe*." I gave him a painful smile. "What's been happening to you?"

There was another exchange of firing and he listened to it intently while I took off my handkerchief and waved it at Bud. I saw him and Bedso start the crew further up the ridge toward the head of the gulley, where they would be able to come down behind the bandits. Then I looked back at Pedro. His eyes were brighter than I'd bet they'd been since he was twenty.

"The General found his men and came back last night," he said. "We had taken the horse herd up the draw on the south of the bowl where the cattle were, the one where the stream comes down and there is some grass. We were asleep. Then we heard the bandits, the shooting and yelling. They came from the east, through the middle of the cattle. Some they ran north, the rest they drove up this canyon. They did not know we were there. That took fine riding, Señor, you must admit. That Huira, he is bad but he is not a fool."

"I agree. It was a slick job, but how did you get here?"

His mouth spread in a grin of child-like delight and he patted his chest. "We, the vaqueros, are smart too. We followed behind the bandits with the horses and in the dark they thought we were some of them. They were happy to have the horses and when the animals were in this canyon and quieted they went up where they are to sleep. It was very late and everybody was tired. We all slept until the sun came over the mountain but we vaqueros waked up first. We stampeded the herd down the hill and when the bandits tried to come down we had them bottled up. We have been keeping them there, waiting for help."

"It's here, Pedro. Your boys, they may be new at the game but they came through just fine."

He glowed for a moment, then sobered in concern. "The cattle that ran north . . . The new Señora—?"

"Is safe and sound in El Paso. Both women are at the hotel."

"And Mike Brown?" There was a grisly hope in his tone.

"Is dead, shot by bandits."

Pedro crossed himself perfunctorily and sighed in relief.

CHAPTER SEVENTEEN

Bud Gilbert with Harry Bedso and his men were by now at the head of the draw, behind the bandits. They left their horses on top and came down the more gentle slope of the side opposite the one I had used, firing a solid volley at Huira's crowd. The vaqueros sent their own volley and General Huira had had enough. A white flag appeared, shaken on the end of a rifle barrel, and I yelled, "Come down here with your hands up. Throw your guns away where I can see them."

Huira stood up, tossed his rifle toward me and came from behind his boulder, walking slowly, suspicious. His ragtag gang came behind him, looking over their shoulders at Bud's crew, crowding them forward. The vaqueros stood up too, with their rifles ready. When the General was close enough that we could see his face plainly he widened his eyes in pretense of astonishment and cried, "Men of Mexico. My own people. Why didn't you call out? I would not have shot had I known."

Without any warning at all Pedro Navarro threw his gun to his shoulder and fired. The bullet took Huira in the chest and when he fell Pedro walked to him and put another through the head.

My breath rushed out. Shooting a man without

a weapon in his hand went against the American grain. It was done and could not be undone but I shouted at him in protest. The young vaqueros swung to look at me with innocent puzzlement on their dark faces and I fell silent. It was their country and they had their own ways, and who was I to interfere. Besides, we needed them, few and inexperienced as they were.

Pedro turned to me with injured dignity and said in Spanish so the boys would understand, "Señor Stewart, in America you have a strong government and soldiers who obey it. In this poor land we have no protection from such as Huira. We must protect ourselves. He tricked you once. For a long time he has deserved to be executed and that is what I have done. Also I have killed him quickly, without pain. He did not dangle from a rope as the condemned do in your country."

Then he forgot me and ordered his boys to take the bandits' other weapons and bandoliers, leaving only a knife for each five men, then to walk them up to the ridge and start them down the far side, watching to make sure they went south.

Bud's group came on slowly as the bandits were herded through them, the American outlaws eyeing the *Jefe* with an expression that was almost respect. It made me wonder if Navarro's brand of justice might not be what was needed to handle the Bedso and Curly Bill crews if they tried to steal the Livingstone herd.

Bud Gilbert reached me and his wry smile told me he had the same idea, then he bowed to Navarro. I cut in quickly with a report of how the Mexicans had saved this half of the herd and Bud reached for the man's hand.

"My wife and I owe you much, *Jefe*. It will not be forgotten. Now you boys wait up here while we go down and send up some horses for you. It's quite a hike down this hill. Then we'll see how many cows we can find."

We found a lot. They were scattered far and wide in the canyons and brush and for the next three days everybody rode hard to bring them together. When the final count was finished there were over nine thousand steers, an amazing salvage considering that they had been through two stampedes and the pile-up in the river.

Billy Lee Parks came into El Paso but neither Bud nor I went anywhere near him until we were sure of the tally. Then, since I had had contact with him, Bud delegated me to do the original bargaining. The gross man was in a genial mood, stuffing himself with a steak as big as the platter it lay on.

"Come in, Cactus." He beckoned with the fork almost hidden in his left fist. "That faro bank—Harry tells me Bert out-slickered you. But thanks for telling me about his skimming. I've got him straightened out along that line."

"That isn't all I hold against Thorne," I said. If Bedso had told him about the bank he would also have reported on Thorne's letter, so there wasn't any use in pretense, and I wanted to find out Parks' reaction.

The politician belched, shoved another bite in his mouth, chewed it and swallowed. "So Whitey says. I don't like my people doing things like that behind my back. That what you came to see me about?"

"No." I hadn't been invited but I took the chair across the table. "I came about the herd. With Curly Bill dead your arrangement with him is over. You need to make a new deal."

The fat man pursed his lips. "And where do you fit into such a deal?"

"I'm representing Bud Gilbert and his wife, who owns the Livingstone ranch, and neither of them has any agreement with you. You've been buying stock from Curly Bill for half what it's worth and they want a better shake."

Billy Lee began to laugh, a truly frightening sight. He shook from his hair to his shoes with such a monstrous quaking that I expected him to split his skin and ooze all over the place. Then he began talking in gasps between his rumbles.

"I like you, Stewart. You've got more gall than sense. First you con me into giving you a faro bank you can't handle and now you think you can hold me up for those mangy cows. Well sir, I've lived a long time and a lot of folks have tried to get the best of poor old Billy Lee. There's not one of them has done it, no siree. I'm not a man to brag, but nobody ever did beat me in a business deal.

"Now you listen here. There's nine thousand head of cattle that's been driven near a hundred miles. Been stampeded twice so most of what little fat they had on them is run off. If I don't buy them, and I'm not sure I want to now, what do you do with them? Drive them back to the ranch? Nobody else in Texas or Arizona will pay any more for them than I will. There's plenty of cattle up here already, for higher prices, and I'm the only market big enough to take your herd. You can't sit where you are and sell them piecemeal because there's not enough grass for more than a week. Besides, I can pull off both American crews. Then where are you?"

Bud and I had already talked all this over and it was perfectly true. He and Anne Marie were at the mercy of this boss unless I could run a pretty good bluff, which I meant to do. I gave him an easy smile.

"We drive them up into Arizona where Bud Gilbert's father has a place." I didn't say the place was a hotel, not a ranch, and I doubted that with all his web of informers he would know much about a dot on the map named Silver. "We'll hold them there, put some fat on and then drive on into Colorado. They're yelling for cattle for the new mining camps."

Billy Lee looked startled. He didn't like that prospect at all. Then he got his composure back.

"Who you counting on to do the driving? Two men and a girl? Curly Bill's crew don't dare set a foot in the states and Whitey Bedso's men take my orders. You think I'd send them with you?"

"We don't need them." I sat back and crossed one leg over my knee to look as casual and confident as I could. "We've got twenty vaqueros who learned how to drive a herd and handle a stampede, and we won't be jumped by more rustlers than we can take. Those boys proved themselves as fighters just the other day . . . I'll lay some cards on the table." I didn't want to crowd him into a corner, wanted to leave him an out. "I don't imagine you know it, but when Curly Bill was killed Harry Bedso got a notion he could move in and grab the herd for nothing. He's underestimating the vaqueros. His and Curly Bill's crews only fight because they're paid, but the Mexicans will fight for their patroness because if she can't keep the ranch going they lose their homes. Believe me, if you go that route there are going to be a lot of dead riders."

His eyes almost disappeared in the folds of fat

as he narrowed them, managing at the same time to look hurt.

"You ought to run for office, Stewart. You make a good speech."

I hadn't suspected him of having any humor and I didn't have to fake my laugh. Then his innocent act came.

"But you don't think I'd go along with Bedso, steal from a woman?"

I looked straight at him. "If you thought you could get away with it, yes."

Again the huge body shook dangerously. "You don't pull any punches, do you? Well now, have you got the authority to agree to a price?"

"I have." I was over the big hurdle. He would buy. The next job was to get enough out of him to cover up my bluff without asking so much that he'd back off. "I won't hold you up, Billy Lee. As you say, the herd isn't in the best condition. You would have paid Brocious half what the steers are worth but we'll settle for three quarters."

He really shocked me then. I expected him to haggle dollar by dollar but he said without hesitation, "I'll split the difference with you. I can pass that along when I sell. Fifteen dollars a head."

"I'll take it."

I stood to leave. He would double the money, get thirty from the contractors, but it was even a better deal for Anne Marie and Bud. With that much money they could hire an American fighting crew who were not outlaws and by paying them on Brocious's high scale draw the top hands. Bud had plans already formed. If Billy Lee Parks had chosen to steal the herd, there wasn't a thing we could have done about it. Our twenty vaqueros could not have stood up against the double crew of hardcases as I claimed, but now Bud intended training his Mexicans, drilling them into the high-quality, competent crew they were capable of being and adding to their numbers from the scattered men who had worked the vandalized ranches until they could ward off the biggest raiding armies themselves.

I had started for the door when Billy Lee called me back.

"Cactus," he said, "Harry told me about your father in Yuma. He was a damn fool to do that for any woman, but I could help get him out. I thought you'd ask me to."

A warning like the buzz of a snake rang in my head and I knew I had to be very careful here. I said, "Why would you want to help me or him? What could you do?"

He showed me the benign face of a ward heeler, tipping his swollen head on one side and smiling.

"I told you I liked you. You've got the guts I admire, and you must know I have some influence in the state capital. Just let me take that letter Thorne wrote and I'll show it to the

Governor and he'll pardon your father right away."

Sure you would, I thought. Just let you get your hands on that letter and it would be burned before I closed the door after me. He had said he did not like his people committing murders and being paid for them behind his back. He was not getting a cut of the price. And he would not want evidence like that floating around among people who could tie Thorne to him. On second thought, he probably wouldn't burn the letter but confront Thorne with it and want his share of the five thousand. But I looked at him eagerly.

"That's mighty generous of you, Billy Lee, but I haven't got it on me. I could bring it tomorrow—"

"You do that."

He beamed on me and flapped a hand at me as I went out the door.

I hunted up Bud Gilbert right away, found him and Anne Marie on horses south of the river, waiting for my report, and told them about the sale of the herd. The girl looked as happy as I had ever seen her. She would get from this herd more than twice what she had under Bill Brocious's stewardship and she was embarrassing in her thanks.

"Go get the money now, both of you," I told them. "Put most of it in an American bank. Anne Marie, in Texas the same as in Mexico a husband has control of a wife's property, so take good care of Bud." I told them about Billy Lee wanting to get hold of Thorne's letter. "So I'm going to ride out before he sends Whitey Bedso to try to get it."

Bud Gilbert offered his hand in sober silence. He and I had ridden a lot of trails together and who knew when or where we would meet again. I thought how different it could have been for me if there hadn't been my father's trouble, if I could have met Anne Marie under different circumstances. But then I would probably never have met her at all.

She put her horse around Bud's to my side, facing me, and laid a hand on my arm, tightening her fingers and sending a tingling all through me.

"After you get your father out of Yuma what will you do, Sam?"

I could hardly bear to look at her while she was this close. "Go back to gambling, I guess. Move around."

"Oh, don't. You're too good a man to waste yourself at a card table. When you're free come back down to the ranch. We'll need a foreman."

Without warning she leaned across and kissed me. It was the only chance I would ever have and I pulled her close and kissed her back, really kissed her. When I let her go she flushed and I turned to Bud. He was grinning from ear to ear, not at all worried. While we looked at each other we knew that the Flying L would not be on my path. Bud was my friend, the best friend a man ever had, and a woman, any woman, has a way of coming between friends.

"Luck, both of you," I said. "So long."

CHAPTER EIGHTEEN

While they rode across to collect from Billy Lee Parks I went for my gear, wondering if either of them was prepared to be confronted by the fat man. I was confident that Parks would pay off as long as he expected me to bring him Thorne's letter, but I was pretty sure he wouldn't if he knew he wasn't going to get it.

I stayed around El Paso until I saw Anne Marie, looking very dazed, and Bud, with something like shock on his face, come out of the hotel and go directly to the bank. I was in Dave Hood's office showing him the Thorne letter and telling him where he could find the remains of Curly Bill Brocious. He wasn't excited about either.

"Let's forget Brocious," he said. "He's dead now, which is all that matters to me. As to Thorne, I wish I could help but murder is a problem for the local Territorial authorities, not for the federal government. But in Tombstone look up Walter Small. He's the new Deputy U.S. Marshal for the southern district of Arizona and he might be able to pin some federal offense on Thorne."

That was a setback I hadn't counted on and I didn't like what it pointed to, that I might have to rely on Billy Lee after all, find some lever to make him deliver, though I hadn't any idea what it might be. Whatever, I first had to get hold of Bert Thorne.

I rode to Benton, left my horse at the livery and caught the stage into Tombstone. It dropped me off at Allen and I walked to the Russ House where Nellie Cashman welcomed me like it was old home day, coming out from behind the desk and taking both my hands.

"How nice to have you back, Mr. Stewart. You didn't stay with us long last time."

"I had some business to take care of. You got room for me?"

"Surely. Do you want a bed for Bud Gilbert too?"

"Not this trip. Bud got married—to the owner of one of the biggest ranches in Chihuahua."

Her fine eyes rounded and she laughed. "Of course he would."

"What's that mean?"

"Why, he was always so flashy and gallant, the type that attracts women. Is she pretty or just rich?"

"That's not kind, and she's beautiful, a lovely girl."

I spoke with more feeling than I intended and she gave me a sharp glance before she handed me a pen to sign the ledger and went to take a key from the board.

With her back to me she said, "You ought to

be married too, Mr. Stewart. A good wife would settle you down."

I chuckled. "A gambling man makes a poor husband. There's not much security for a woman."

Why did all women want to marry off the single men? Especially this one, who had never married herself? Whatever story lay behind that intrigued me, for she had had many offers in Tombstone and I felt sure there had been others in the list of camps where she had run boarding houses, but I did not feel privileged to ask. I went up to the hot, close room, cleaned up and shaved and put on a clean shirt. Then I went looking for Walter Small's office above Hatche's hardware store on Tough Nut Street.

The marshal was as tall a man as I had met in many a day, the size who are always the butt of cracks about the weather up there, but looking into his deep blue eyes I decided that anyone who kidded him was a prize damn fool.

I said, "My name's Sam Stewart. Dave Hood over at El Paso told me to see you."

He stood up to shake hands, then folded himself into his chair again. "Mr. Stewart. What can I do for you?"

"Probably nothing, Marshal, unless as Hood suggested you might have a reason, even a very slight one, to arrest a man here in town."

It was not the smartest way I could have put it. The eyes turned to ice at the hint that he might not have arrested someone he should have. I went on in a hurry with the story of my father and what I had done so far. When I spoke of meeting Curly Bill Brocious he forgot about being offended and leaned forward against the desk, his voice snapping.

"Brocious is alive?"

"Not now. He was until a few days ago, but I watched him buried just south of the border."

He sank back and listened while I went through the rest of it. When I showed him the letter from Bert Thorne he read it and flicked it with a forefinger, making a wry mouth.

"Yes, that's Thorne. I've seen that thumb scar. But I haven't anything on him, and anyway you're too late. He pulled out of town night before last. His partner told me he wouldn't be back."

I focused on a dirty spot on the wall behind the marshal, my voice dull. "I suppose you don't know where he went?"

Of course Small shook his head. So Thorne had been warned that I was coming after him, and the warning could only have been sent by Harry Bedso or Billy Lee Parks. No one else except Bud Gilbert and his wife knew it, and I would suspect myself before I would them. A gone feeling pushed me against the chair back. I had been so close. And being so close had blinded me. I had kidded myself that Billy Lee was put out with Thorne enough to intercede with the Governor.

Now I was in effect back where I started. I put my hands on the chair arms and shoved to my feet, feeling the full, heavy weight of my body.

"Thank you for your trouble. And keep that letter for me, will you?"

"I will. Sorry I can't be more help."

I went down the outside stairs, every step down the splintered and weathered treads jarring clear up through my chin. I still had to find Thorne and the only lead I knew was James Markley. In my present mood I would thoroughly enjoy beating what I wanted out of him.

It was still two hours before dark and Tough Nut Street was full with the usual afternoon crowd, the Turquoise Palace already jammed. All the gambling tables were running and it took muscle to work through to the bar. When I made it a bartender I remembered from the earlier times I had spent in town poured a glass of whiskey without asking, saying he was glad to see me back.

"Thanks," I said. "Markley in the office?"

"Yep."

"I hear Bert Thorne isn't around anymore."

A veil dropped over his eyes and he moved quickly away. I threw my drink down and needed another, but the bartender apparently didn't see my signal, didn't come near me. I shrugged, spun a coin on the counter, and went back through the press using my shoulders as roughly as Bud did until I reached the office door and tried it. It was not locked and I shoved it open.

Markley was writing in a ledger at the desk and his eyes came up when he heard the door. A strained expression tightened his face but he did not pretend to be surprised and his voice was wary.

"Hello, Cactus."

I shut the door behind me and prowled to the desk, my gun leveled on him. "Put your hands on the desk, flat."

Slowly he spread them out, palms down and fingers splayed.

I said, "Where is Bert Thorne? Who warned him I was coming?"

"I couldn't say."

I reached over and raked my gunsight across one cheek, cutting it. He gasped and started to stand up. I shoved him down, hard.

"That's for openers. I want Thorne. Where is he?"

Sweat broke out on his forehead and he lifted one hand to the blood starting from the cut. "I don't—"

"Stop it. You do know. You're his partner and he wouldn't go off without telling you where to find him."

His eyes went past me to the door but I didn't fall for the trick and he said in a nervous tone, "I really don't—"

I hit him again, this time above the ear. I was careful not to knock him out but the blow brought tears to his eyes and he squinted them shut, shook his head, and put up a bent arm across his face.

"No more, Cactus. I tell you I—"

"Lay your hands back on that desk. I am going to break your fingers one at a time until you tell me."

Instead he doubled his fists, pressing them against his chest, saying faintly, "I believe you would. You're crazy enough."

"And mad enough."

His face broke up like a blubbering kid and his head bobbed. "Don't. Please. Bert's hiding out at the old Potter place."

"Where is it?"

"On the Gettysville-Charleston road, about six miles from Charleston."

I recognized the location then, an old ranch the Clantons had holed up in more than once. I hit Markley once more behind the ear and this time he toppled forward on the desk, out cold. I found a ball of thick twine in a drawer, tied his hands and ankles, and stuffed a gag in his mouth and tied it. Someone would find him sooner or later but I wanted an hour's start. I didn't want him in a position to try to stop me or get a message to Thorne.

I went back through the saloon as unobtrusively as I could and down to the livery to rent a horse. Mounting, I started to turn southwest for Charleston, then I thought of something else and rode to the telegraph office.

The clerk was more than half asleep. The instrument was clattering but his call letters were so branded in his brain that he could doze and still know when a message for this station came through. I slammed the door to wake him and when he looked up I said, "I want to see the files of messages you received day before yesterday and since."

His eyebrows popped up on his forehead as he straightened. "Oh . . . You can't. That's against the regulations."

He was a nervous, jumpy, stooped man. I lifted my gun and showed it to him. "Does this change the regulations?"

He swallowed, staring at the gun, and stammered. "Why, yes sir. I guess maybe it does. I'll get them right away."

He swiveled to a safe behind his table, took a spindle with a stack of yellow papers spiked on it from the top and swung back, shoving it toward me. I put the gun away and thumbed through the messages and found one addressed to Bert Thorne that read:

SAM STEWART WISE. HAS LETTER YOU WROTE MIKE BROWN. SUGGEST YOU MAKE TRACKS.

But it was not signed. I shook it at the

clerk, angry that I was blocked at every turn.

"Can you find out who sent this?"

The man tugged at his collar. "I could call the operator at El Paso."

I found a ten-dollar gold piece in my pocket and dropped it before him. "Do that, will you?"

He was quick enough to oblige me then, his finger swift and sure on his key; then we waited while the reply clicked out. When it was finished the clerk shook his head and told me, "He sent the wire, all right, but he didn't know the man who brought it in."

It was useless to ask him to find out if the sender had been a very fat man. Billy Lee Parks would have sent some hireling, not taken the message to the office himself, so I was at another dead end. I went out and swung up on my rented horse.

It was about twelve miles to Charleston and I set the animal down at a steady trot and made the town in two hours. Night came down but a full moon climbed the eastern sky and turned the desert I rode through a dusty silver. Charleston was going full blast, all three mills running at capacity, and the off-shift men filled the deadfalls with a noisy clamor. This had always been an outlaw town—still was, even if some of its more notorious characters were dead or had moved on. I did not stop but rode straight through to the Gettysville road, which dipped south through rough hills, then turned north.

The Potter headquarters was a two-room log cabin built by an early Mormon who had tried to ranch on the San Pedro and not made it. The cabin was in pretty good condition, kept up with minor repairs by the outlaws who stopped there from time to time. There were other buildings they had not bothered to maintain: a hay barn with a roof sagging in the middle, a crooked shed where Potter had sheared the few sheep he ran, a blacksmith shop, and a bunkhouse for the man he used in haying season.

I tied my animal to a gate post at the entrance of the lane and walked the rest of the way so that if there were horses in the corral they wouldn't neigh at a strange one coming in and alert Thorne before I could get to him. This time I had better luck. The moonlight showed me the dark shape of a single horse behind the pole bars.

The yard was quiet, the cabin dark. I moved in silently, watchful, hoping there were no dogs to give me away, my rifle ready, but no shadowy shapes rushed at me. I reached the house and saw that the door was shut but there was no lock, only a simple latch. I lifted it without noise and edged the door open, nosing the gun barrel through.

Enough moonlight filtered in so that I could make out the room, but not clearly enough to see definite objects. There was no sound inside, no movement. I eased through the door and struck a match. The room was empty, the door to the second room closed. It was puzzling. Bert Thorne was a night man, conditioned to running the Turquoise Palace until dawn, and it didn't make sense that he was asleep so early in the evening. But maybe he was bored here all alone, maybe he had drunk himself into a stupor with nothing else to do.

The match showed me a lamp on the table before it burned out. I struck another, lifted the sooted chimney and lit the wick, put the chimney back and catfooted to the inner door. I eased that open and saw bunks against the wall. All of them were empty.

Bert Thorne was not in the cabin, yet there was a horse in the corral. Had he brought an extra and ridden into Gettysville to entertain himself? Or was he in Charleston and had I passed him without knowing it? I swore, wondering how long I would have to wait until he came.

I would have to move my horse, bring it up and tie it behind the cabin, and I turned back to the open outer door. I was reaching for the lamp to douse it when a shot slammed out of the night and shattered it, showering me with glass splinters.

I dropped to the floor and used my sleeve to beat out the flame that licked up in the spilled oil, and lay in the dark cursing myself. Like some stupid, green kid I had walked into a trap.

I'd been so intent on finding Thorne, so single-minded, so sure that I had frightened Markley that it had never occurred to me that they might have planned together to send me here.

CHAPTER NINETEEN

Not even the faint rustle of night animals broke the quiet outside. I crawled to the single window in the side wall and looked out. Nothing moved in the area I could see. Whoever had shot was hidden in another building and there was no way to know if it was Thorne. He and Markley might have hired a gunman to get rid of me. Or more than one. There was only one horse in the corral but that could be a plant, and I had to know.

I went to the stove in the kitchen corner and fumbled on the shelf beside it, found an iron skillet and took it back to the door. With my back against the wall I threw the skillet through the window across the room. Before it crashed through the glass I had spun to put an eye around the door jamb.

There were two quick shots, one from the hay barn, the other from the bunkhouse. Thorne, if it was him, was not alone, and for all I knew he could be safe at the Turquoise Palace laughing his head off. I soon had an answer to that question. When the noise of the shots had died, Bert Thorne's voice yelled from the bunkhouse.

"Come on out, Stewart. Give me that letter and we'll let you go."

I kept out of sight and quiet. Let them think one

of the bullets had hit me. I was in no hurry to do anything just yet. The cottonwood walls were thick enough to stop any lead except some lucky shot that might strike the mud-plastered chinks between them. They didn't even try throwing any more. They had me boxed in, and all they had to do was watch that I didn't slip out through the door or window and wait until I needed water enough to panic.

That might be their game but I didn't intend to play it with them and stay there tamely. I studied the door and the angle it made with the bunkhouse and barn. Thorne could cover the door but the man in the barn could not. The window was a different matter. Both men had a clear shot at that, so it was out, and anyway it was framed with jagged glass. If I tried to clean it they could hear me and train both guns on it.

I might try a dash through the door and hope that my sudden appearance would startle Thorne for the second it would take me to be around the corner of the building, that he would not react in time. If I could get around that corner I would have a fighting chance of making the blacksmith shop before they could cut down on me. But would I be any better off there than where I was? I didn't think so and looked for another choice.

The fireplace caught my attention. It was bigmouthed, built of native stone set in mortar that was crumbling. Some of the corner stones had fallen out The fire box was big enough that a man could climb inside it, but could I climb the chimney or would it be too small?

I crawled to it and felt over it in the dark. Ashes of old fires were deep on the hearth. I sat down and hunched in on them, ducking my head to clear the arch, twisting until I could look up the flu. It was thick with scaling soot but at the top the rectangle of pale sky looked ample. I stretched both hands over my head, the rifle in my right, and like a contortionist wriggled to my knees, got a fingerhold in a crack, and pulled myself to my feet. Soot rained down and I kept my head bent and shut my eyes. The fire clay that had lined the box was broken in spots and the rocks behind it were round river stones. I stood on the ashes with my shoulders brushing both inside walls of the chimney and fumbled with a boot toe for a place from which I could lever myself higher. The first one lifted me only a few inches. I hung there, wedged against the wall, feeling over my head for another hold, and when I found a rough rock jutting into the flu, got a grip on that and felt for a second toehold.

Whoever the mason had been, he had done me a favor. The chimney was rough all the way up and cramped enough that I could wedge my feet against one wall, my shoulders against the opposite, and push up an inch at a time. It took a long while and a lot of sweat, and my muscles were shaking involuntarily before I was halfway up. I had to stop and rest, bring my arms down and lie against the wall again and again. My face and hands were greasy with sweat and soot.

It must have been two hours before I could get my fingers over the crown and claw at it. Then I was able to lift the rifle clear and put my right arm over the top and use it to help haul me up the last steps. But as I put pressure on the rock under my left hand it broke out of the old mortar and fell away, landed on my shoulder and bounced off. The sudden release of the tension on my arm almost dropped me back to the bottom, but my right arm held, quivering with tiredness, and my feet kept me braced.

The falling stone clicked against the wall with a dull rattling and landed in the ashes with no more sound. It taught me to be more careful. I did not again trust an individual stone, shoving and pulling until I could hook both elbows over the crown and climb out on my back like a slithering lizard. Fortunately, the chimney was only a foot higher than the roof. With the base of my spine on the crown, I rolled onto my stomach and slid down to the hand-hewn shakes.

The roof had little pitch and I sprawled there, resting, trying to scrub some of the greasy soot from my hands. It was another half hour before I got back the strength to move further, until my legs quit trembling. I lay studying the moonlit yard, seeing no movement in either the bunkhouse or barn and not knowing whether in the long lapse of time Thorne or his gunman had moved closer. They might be against the house by now, might have come into it. But I did not believe that. If they had come in they would have heard me and been waiting in the yard to blow my head off as I squirmed out of the chimney. I lay just under the roof peak, on the side not visible to anyone in the bunkhouse or barn, only the top of my head as far down as my eyes protruding above it against the chimney.

When I felt able, I backed down the shakes and looked over the edge to be sure I didn't land on top of them. The ground was empty and only some seven feet below. I slid my feet over and let myself down until I hung from the eaves, then dropped. I could make the corral unseen from where I was, take the horse standing in it and escape. But that was not what I wanted. I wanted the man who could clear my father.

I could also go around the corral to the blacksmith shop, but one of the men might have moved there. My best bet seemed to be to duck around the rear of the blacksmith shop and go on to the back of the barn. If I could get through a rear door of that I would be behind the gunman, if he was still there.

Hidden by the cabin, I ran for the corral, holding my breath that neither Thorne nor the other had shifted to a place from which they could spot my movement, my back tense to take a bullet. But I reached the barn and there was no shot. One of the doors at the back hung askew on the top hinge, the lower pulled out of the frame. It left a gap through which I could crawl, but first I lay down and looked inside. The runway was black, but at the far end the waning moonlight silhouetted a dark figure sitting on a box in the deep shadow of the entrance, hunched there with a gun across his knees.

I wormed through and knew I was framed in light when he gave a sharp cry.

"Hey..."

I nearly jumped out of my skin. I dropped and rolled, thinking he had seen me, but there was an answering call from the bunkhouse.

"What?"

The man in front of me called, "What's he doing in there all this time?"

"I don't know."

"Maybe we hit him. Maybe he's dead."

"I hope."

"Well, I'm tired of this. I'm going to find out. I can get out the back here and around behind the cabin without him being able to see me. I'll go down the blank side. When I turn the corner to get to the door, cover me."

"All right."

The gunman stood up, turned around and came

toward me, walking fast, his rifle hanging loose in his hand. I waited in the black tunnel of the runway, thanking the luck that had finally sent things my way, waited until he leaned the rifle against the solid door and bent, using both hands to lift the other and shove it out. He never knew what hit him when my gun cracked against his head. He fell silently at my feet. I rolled him over and struck a match, cupping it above the face, and looked down on Harry Bedso.

I could not have been more surprised. I had thought Whitey would still be in Texas supervising the takeover of the herd. I did not waste time thinking about it but shucked out of my coat, took his and put it on, then fumbled until I found his hat. I left the barn and ran to the back of the cabin and down the blank side.

As soon as I reached the corner of the front wall I stepped away from it and waved toward the bunkhouse, and at once Bert Thorne began firing, spacing his shots through the door. You see what you expect to see, and he thought he was covering Whitey. I moved along the wall, took off the hat and put it on the end of my rifle, edging it around the door jamb as if to draw fire from anyone inside, but watching the bunkhouse. Light glinted off Thorne's gun where it poked through a window there. Then I leaned forward as though peering into the dark cabin, straightened confidently and stepped inside.

A minute later I called, "He's dead."

I pressed against the inside wall beside the door and waited, hearing running steps cross the yard, ready to throw down on Thorne as soon as he crossed the threshold. But he did not come directly. He was smarter than I gave him credit for. With my back to the window I heard glass on the ground crack under his foot, spun and saw him standing outside, bringing up his rifle. Whether my voice had made him suspicious or whether he meant to kill Bedso I did not have time to question. He was a trifle late. My shot caught him in the throat just before he fired and his bullet went wild.

I went outside to look at him. He was dead. I hadn't meant to kill him, had wanted him alive to beat a confession out of, but only his head and neck had been visible and it was a choice of him or me.

His body was no good to me. Marshal Small had already recognized the scarred thumbprint on the letter, but now what could I do? Where could I turn to get my father out of Yuma?

I went back to the barn, where Bedso was still unconscious, tied his hands and feet, then found a shovel and buried Thorne. By the time I was finished Bedso had waked and lay fighting the ropes and swearing viciously. I pulled the broken door wide so he could see and recognize me, and when he did he cursed me too.

"How the hell could you pull this?"

"I'm smarter than you. I just buried Bert Thorne. Here are his watch and rings."

He looked at them in my hand and shrugged.

I said, "You are going to join him unless you spill your guts quick. What are you doing here?"

He gave a sour laugh. "I'd get myself killed telling you."

"You surely will if you don't." I took out my short gun.

"So what's the difference? Kid, you used to be all right. You wouldn't shoot a man trussed up like this."

I wouldn't, and I wasn't going to get anything out of him here. "Billy Lee sent you, didn't he? He didn't want me loose with Thorne's letter to take to the newspapers and open up a scandal that could force the Governor to free my father. It might nick into his power if someone could get anything out of the capital without him."

The way his eyes changed told me I had guessed right, and now a new way to go was opened to me. I crouched and untied his feet with one hand, keeping the gun in the other, then stood back and told him to get up and walk to the corral. He got to his feet, suspicious.

"What do you think you're going to do now?"

"Take you to Tombstone and beat some answers out of you. Listen good now, Whitey, you make one squawk when we get to Charleston I'll shoot you out of the saddle."

He gave me a crafty glance and headed for the corral and the horse there. I knew he was thinking of getting help in Tombstone, but I had a surprise for him that I wouldn't tell him because I wanted him to ride willingly, not go through the outlaw town with ropes on. I took his short gun, then freed his wrists and told him to saddle the horse they had left for bait. I mounted that and made him walk ahead of me out to the gate and get on my rented animal, then we set out single file, Whitey in front where I could watch him.

Bedso behaved himself passing through Charleston and on along toward Tombstone. Two miles short of there Chald Bryan and his two brothers ran a small dairy. They bottled their milk in old whiskey bottles and sold them for a dollar apiece. I had taught them how to play poker and watch for a crooked deal and I thought they would look after my prisoner for a couple of hours. He cursed us all while we tied him to a post in the milking shed, then I rode on to the marshal's office. Small came back to the dairy with me and I told Bedso to start talking. He didn't want to but after I worked him over for a while he changed his mind.

What he told was the whole story of the Tucson Ring. He really laid it out and even Small was shocked. I wrote it down as he told it and when he finished he signed it and Small signed as witness. Then we let him go. The last I saw of Whitey Bedso he was heading for the Mexican border as fast as the horse could take him.

Small watched after him with smoking eyes, then sighed. There wasn't anything a federal officer could hold him on. He said, "You going to turn that paper over to the government?"

"Why?"

"It proves the army's being cheated on the beef contracts and the state politics are rotten."

"Who in Washington do you think would pay any real attention?"

He shrugged, knowing as well as I that corruption was rife in very high places. "What do you want it for then?"

"To throw a scare into a fat man. Billy Lee can't be sure the attorney general wouldn't land on him. I'm going to trade it for a pardon. Thank you for your help."

We rode back to Tombstone and I caught the stage. Parks was back in Tucson and a man I hadn't seen before was on the gate. I told him to tell Billy Lee I had brought Bert Thorne's letter and he came back on the run to let me in.

Billy Lee was eating as usual, or had been. He sat in the big chair as if he were looking at a ghost, staring without a word. I sat down opposite him and let him have it fast.

"I'm just back from Tombstone. Bert Thorne

is dead." I flipped the watch and rings across the table. "Whitey Bedso left for Mexico, but before he went he signed this."

I spread the paper in front of him and he read it, his face turning a dark purple.

I said, "I have a gun on you under this table. Don't call anybody."

"Who . . . who's this Small that witnessed it?"

"Don't stall, Billy Lee, you know every officer in Arizona. He's a U.S. marshal. You shouldn't have crossed me up. Now I'll give you one last chance to get that pardon for my father. If you don't I'll take that thing to the President of the United States if I have to ride a horse into the White House."

He mopped at his neck and forehead. "You've done everything else you said you would. You're hell on wheels, aren't you? What if I do what you want?"

"You can have the paper."

He raised his voice and bellowed for paper and pen and when a Mexican woman brought them to the patio he wrote to the Governor. While he was writing I put the Bedso story in my pocket. He signed his note, pushed it toward me and held his hand out.

"There you are. Gimme that damned thing."

I folded the note and put it with the confession. "I'll mail it to you when Rob Stewart is released."

He didn't want it that way. He knew all about double-crosses—and accidents.

"Don't mail it. Bring it yourself. Do that and I can use you, but if I don't get it there's no place you can hide where I won't find you."

I laughed aloud. "Don't worry so much, Billy Lee. Everybody doesn't think like you do."

I stood up, letting him see the gun while I put it in my pocket and kept my hand on it. I backed to the gate, where the man let me out and locked it after me, and Billy Lee didn't make a sound.

I rode to Prescott and delivered his note. It was frightening how fast the pardon was forthcoming. I was on my way to Yuma in a quarter of an hour.

The warden had my father brought to his office. Rob Stewart's back was still ramrod straight but his face was haggard, his eyes dull. He looked clear through me and I wanted to weep for him. The warden handed him the pardon without speaking. He took it hesitantly, as if he were afraid of what it might be, but as he read it he brushed at his eyes and when he looked up there were tears there.

"Sam . . . You didn't involve—"

"No," I said quickly. "I learned that a man named Bert Thorne killed Danby and went to the Governor with the proof. You should never have confessed to a crime you didn't commit."

He looked at me through a long silence, sighing. "Sam, have you been in love yet?"

Anne Marie's shining face hung in the air between us and I nodded slowly.

"I wasn't as lucky as you. Bud Gilbert got her. There's a horse outside for you and I'll ride partway to Lordsburg with you."

We went out and rode away from Yuma prison. He seemed to throw off years as we talked, as I told him what I had done since I had last seen him. At the branch road we shook hands and I turned north, toward Montana. That was about as far away as I could get from Chihuahua.

Center Point Large Print
600 Brooks Road / PO Box 1
Thorndike, ME 04986-0001 USA

(207) 568-3717

US & Canada:
1 800 929-9108
www.centerpointlargeprint.com